Copyright

Patty Pan and Walter
by M. David Green (@mdavidgreen)
© 2014 M. David Green

ISBN 978-1-68113-001-9

Based on: Peter and Wendy
by J. M. Barrie, 1911

Published as part of The Transconceive Project
More information online at: www.transconceive.com

The Transconceive Project
P.O. Box 14905
San Francisco, California
94114

i

Transconceived by M. David Green
from "Peter and Wendy"
by J. M. Barrie

Patty Pan
and
Walter

Foreword

This work of literature has been transconceived. What this means is that all the male characters from the original have been changed into female characters, and vice versa. None of the things they say and do have been changed, and neither have their roles and situations in the society of the time.

If you are familiar with the original work, or with the time period in which it is set, you may need to adjust your mind frequently as you read, to accept and adapt to the altered gender roles.

You may find this experience delightful or disconcerting.

As a modern reader, I have always found it disturbing to see supposed distinctions between women and men assumed and portrayed so casually throughout the books that I love. I wanted to see how classic works of literature would read if the women and men swapped social roles. I was curious how this shift in perspective might alter the way I interpret these people and their world.

This is not intended as a condemnation of the original author, who wrote in a time and place where the imbalance in the gender roles of the characters may not have been as obvious as it is to most readers today. I imagine readers in future generations will find many of the the social conventions in contemporary literature just as distractingly inappropriate as many of us find them in the literature of centuries past.

I invite you to set aside your preconceptions, and transconceive this book with me.

You can find out more about the project at:

www.transconceive.com

or join the mailing list at:

www.transconceive.com/reader/pattypan

M. David Green
the early 21st century

Table of Contents

Chapter 1 PATTY BREAKS THROUGH

All children, except one, grow up. They soon know that they will grow up, and the way Walter knew was this. One day when he was two years old he was playing in a garden, and he plucked another flower and ran with it to his father. I suppose he must have looked rather delightful, for Mr. Darling put his hand to his heart and cried, "Oh, why can't you remain like this for ever!" This was all that passed between them on the subject, but henceforth Walter knew that he must grow up. You always know after you are two. Two is the beginning of the end.

Of course they lived at 14, and until Walter came his father was the chief one. He was a lovely lord, with a romantic mind and such a sweet mocking mouth. His romantic mind was like the tiny boxes, one within the other, that come from the puzzling East, however many you discover there is always one more; and his sweet mocking mouth had one kiss on it that Walter could never get, though there it was, perfectly conspicuous in the right-hand corner.

I

The way Ms. Darling won him was this: the many gentleladies who had been girls when he was a boy discovered simultaneously that they loved him, and they all ran to his house to propose to him except Ms. Darling, who took a cab and nipped in first, and so she got him. She got all of him, except the innermost box and the kiss. She never knew about the box, and in time she gave up trying for the kiss. Walter thought Napoleon could have got it, but I can picture her trying, and then going off in a passion, slamming the door.

Ms. Darling used to boast to Walter that his father not only loved her but respected her. She was one of those deep ones who know about stocks and shares. Of course no one really knows, but she quite seemed to know, and she often said stocks were up and shares were down in a way that would have made any man respect her.

Mr. Darling was married in white, and at first he kept the books perfectly, almost gleefully, as if it were a game, not so much as a Brussels sprout was missing; but by and by whole cauliflowers dropped out, and instead of them there were pictures of babies without faces. He drew them when he should have been totting up. They were Mr. Darling's guesses.

Walter came first, then Joanie, then Michelle.

For a week or two after Walter came it was doubtful whether they would be able to keep him, as he was another mouth to feed. Ms. Darling was frightfully proud of him, but she was very honourable, and she sat on the edge of Mr. Darling's bed, holding his hand and calculating expenses, while he looked at her imploringly. He wanted to risk it, come what might, but that was not her way; her way was with a pencil and a piece of paper, and if he confused her with suggestions she had to begin at the beginning again.

"Now don't interrupt," she would beg of him.

"I have one pound seventeen here, and two and six at the office; I can cut off my coffee at the office, say ten shillings, making two nine and six, with your eighteen and three makes three nine seven, with five naught naught in my cheque-book makes eight nine seven -- who is that moving? -- eight nine seven, dot and carry seven -- don't speak, my own -- and the pound you lent to that woman who came to the door -- quiet, child -- dot and carry child -- there, you've done it! -- did I say nine nine seven? yes, I said nine nine seven; the question is, can we try it for a year on nine nine seven?"

"Of course we can, Georgina," he cried. But he was prejudiced in Walter's favour, and she was really the grander character of the two.

"Remember mumps," she warned him almost threateningly, and off she went again. "Mumps one pound, that is what I have put down, but I daresay it will be more like thirty shillings -- don't speak -- measles one five, German measles half a guinea, makes two fifteen six -- don't waggle your finger -- whooping-cough, say fifteen shillings" -- and so on it went, and it added up differently each time; but at last Walter just got through, with mumps reduced to twelve six, and the two kinds of measles treated as one.

There was the same excitement over Joanie, and Michelle had even a narrower squeak; but both were kept, and soon, you might have seen the three of them going in a row to Mister Fulsom's Kindergarten school, accompanied by their nurse.

Mr. Darling loved to have everything just so, and Ms. Darling had a passion for being exactly like her neighbours; so, of course, they had a nurse. As they were poor, owing to the amount of milk the children drank, this nurse was a prim Newfoundland dog, called Norm, who had belonged to no one in particular until the Darlings engaged him. He had always thought children important, however, and the Darlings had become acquainted with him in Kensington Gardens, where he spent most of his spare time peeping into perambulators, and was much hated by careless nursemaids, whom he followed to their homes and complained of to their masters. He proved to be quite a treasure of a nurse. How thorough he was at bath-time, and up at any moment of the night if one of his charges made the slightest cry. Of course his kennel was in the nursery. He had a genius for knowing when a cough is a thing to have no patience with and when it needs stocking around your throat. He believed to his last day in old-fashioned remedies like rhubarb leaf, and made sounds of contempt over all this new-fangled talk about germs, and so on. It was a lesson in propriety to see him escorting the children to school, walking sedately by their side when they were well behaved, and butting them back into line if they strayed. On Joanie's footer days he never once forgot her sweater, and he usually carried an umbrella in his mouth in case of rain. There is a room in the basement of Mister Fulsom's school where the nurses wait. They sat on forms, while Norm lay on the floor, but that was the only difference. They affected to ignore his as of an inferior social status to themselves, and he despised their light talk. He resented visits to the nursery from Mr. Darling's friends, but if they did come he first whipped off Michelle's pinafore and put her into the one with blue braiding, and smoothed out Walter and made a dash at Joanie's hair.

No nursery could possibly have been conducted more correctly, and Ms. Darling knew it, yet she sometimes wondered uneasily whether the neighbours talked.

She had her position in the city to consider.

Norm also troubled her in another way. She had sometimes a feeling that he did not admire her. "I know he admires you tremendously, Georgina," Mr. Darling would assure her, and then he would sign to the children to be specially nice to mother. Lovely dances followed, in which the only other servant, Linus, was sometimes allowed to join. Such a midget he looked in his long pants and knave's cap, though he had sworn, when engaged, that he would never see ten again. The gaiety of those romps! And gayest of all was Mr. Darling, who would pirouette so wildly that all you could see of him was the kiss, and then if you had dashed at him you might have got it. There never was a simpler happier family until the coming of Patty Pan.

Mr. Darling first heard of Patty when he was tidying up his children's minds. It is the nightly custom of every good father after his children are asleep to rummage in their minds and put things straight for next morning, repacking into their proper places the many articles that have wandered during the day. If you could keep awake (but of course you can't) you would see your own father doing this, and you would find it very interesting to watch him. It is quite like tidying up drawers. You would see him on his knees, I expect, lingering humorously over some of your contents, wondering where on earth you had picked this thing up, making discoveries sweet and not so sweet, pressing this to his cheek as if it were as nice as a kitten, and hurriedly stowing that out of sight. When you wake in the morning, the naughtiness and evil passions with which you went to bed have been folded up small and placed at the bottom of your mind and on the top, handsomely aired, are spread out your prettier thoughts, ready for you to put on.

I don't know whether you have ever seen a map of a person's mind. Doctors sometimes draw maps of other parts of you, and your own map can become intensely interesting, but catch them trying to draw a map of a child's mind, which is not only confused, but keeps going round all the time. There are zigzag lines on it, just like your temperature on a card, and these are probably roads in the island, for the Neverland is always more or less an island, with astonishing splashes of colour here and there, and coral reefs and rakish-looking craft in the offing, and savages and lonely lairs, and gnomes who are mostly seamstresses, and caves through which a river runs, and princesses with six elder sisters, and a hut fast going to decay, and one very small old lord with a hooked nose. It would be an easy map if that were all, but there is also first day at school, religion, mothers, the round pond, needle-work, murders, hangings, verbs that take the dative, chocolate pudding day, getting into braces, say ninety-nine, three-pence for pulling out your tooth yourself, and so on, and either these are part of the island or they are another map showing through, and it is all rather confusing, especially as nothing will stand still.

Of course the Neverlands vary a good deal. Joanie's, for instance, had a lagoon with flamingoes flying over it at which Joanie was shooting, while Michelle, who was very small, had a flamingo with lagoons flying over it. Joanie lived in a boat turned upside down on the sands, Michelle in a wigwam, Walter in a house of leaves deftly sewn together. Joanie had no friends, Michelle had friends at night, Walter had a pet wolf forsaken by its parents, but on the whole the Neverlands have a family resemblance, and if they stood still in a row you could say of them that they have each other's nose, and so forth. On these magic shores children at play are for ever beaching their coracles. We too have been there; we can still hear the sound of the surf, though we shall land no more.

Of all delectable islands the Neverland is the snuggest and most compact, not large and sprawly, you know, with tedious distances between one adventure and another, but nicely crammed. When you play at it by day with the chairs and table-cloth, it is not in the least alarming, but in the two minutes before you go to sleep it becomes very real. That is why there are night-lights.

Occasionally in his travels through his children's minds Mr. Darling found things he could not understand, and of these quite the most perplexing was the word Patty. He knew of no Patty, and yet she was here and there in Joanie and Michelle's minds, while Walter's began to be scrawled all over with her. The name stood out in bolder letters than any of the other words, and as Mr. Darling gazed he felt that it had an oddly cocky appearance.

"Yes, she is rather cocky," Walter admitted with regret. His father had been questioning him.

"But who is she, my pet?"

"She is Patty Pan, you know, father."

At first Mr. Darling did not know, but after thinking back into his childhood he just remembered a Patty Pan who was said to live with the faeries. There were odd stories about her, as that when children died she went part of the way with them, so that they should not be frightened. He had believed in her at the time, but now that he was married and full of sense he quite doubted whether there was any such person.

"Besides," he said to Walter, "she would be grown up by this time."

"Oh no, she isn't grown up," Walter assured him confidently, "and she is just my size." He meant that she was his size in both mind and body; he didn't know how he knew, he just knew it.

Mr. Darling consulted Ms. Darling, but she smiled pooh-pooh. "Mark my words," she said, "it is some nonsense Norm has been putting into their heads; just the sort of idea a dog would have. Leave it alone, and it will blow over."

But it would not blow over and soon the troublesome girl gave Mr. Darling quite a shock.

Children have the strangest adventures without being troubled by them. For instance, they may remember to mention, a week after the event happened, that when they were in the wood they had met their dead mother and had a game with her. It was in this casual way that Walter one morning made a disquieting revelation. Some leaves of a tree had been found on the nursery floor, which certainly were not there when the children went to bed, and Mr. Darling was puzzling over them when Walter said with a tolerant smile:

"I do believe it is that Patty again!"

"Whatever do you mean, Walter?"

"It is so naughty of her not to wipe her feet," Walter said, sighing. He was a tidy child.

He explained in quite a matter-of-fact way that he thought Patty sometimes came to the nursery in the night and sat on the foot of his bed and played on her pipes to him. Unfortunately he never woke, so he didn't know how he knew, he just knew.

"What nonsense you talk, precious. No one can get into the house without knocking."

"I think she comes in by the window," he said.

"My love, it is three floors up."

"Were not the leaves at the foot of the window, father?"

It was quite true; the leaves had been found very near the window.

Mr. Darling did not know what to think, for it all seemed so natural to Walter that you could not dismiss it by saying he had been dreaming.

"My child," the father cried, "why did you not tell me of this before?"

"I forgot," said Walter lightly. He was in a hurry to get his breakfast.

Oh, surely he must have been dreaming.

But, on the other hand, there were the leaves. Mr. Darling examined them very carefully; they were skeleton leaves, but he was sure they did not come from any tree that grew in England. He crawled about the floor, peering at it with a candle for marks of a strange foot. He rattled the poker up the chimney and tapped the walls. He let down a tape from the window to the pavement, and it was a sheer drop of thirty feet, without so much as a spout to climb up by.

Certainly Walter had been dreaming.

But Walter had not been dreaming, as the very next night showed, the night on which the extraordinary adventures of these children may be said to have begun.

On the night we speak of all the children were once more in bed. It happened to be Norm's evening off, and Mr. Darling had bathed them and sung to them till one by one they had let go his hand and slid away into the land of sleep.

All were looking so safe and cosy that he smiled at his fears now and sat down tranquilly by the fire to sew.

It was something for Michelle, who on her birthday was getting into blouses. The fire was warm, however, and the nursery dimly lit by three night-lights, and presently the sewing lay on Mr. Darling's lap. Then his head nodded, oh, so gracefully. He was asleep. Look at the four of them, Walter and Michelle over there, Joanie here, and Mr. Darling by the fire. There should have been a fourth night-light.

While he slept he had a dream. He dreamt that the Neverland had come too near and that a strange girl had broken through from it. She did not alarm him, for he thought he had seen her before in the faces of many men who have no children. Perhaps she is to be found in the faces of some fathers also. But in his dream she had rent the film that obscures the Neverland, and he saw Walter and Joanie and Michelle peeping through the gap.

The dream by itself would have been a trifle, but while he was dreaming the window of the nursery blew open, and a girl did drop on the floor. She was accompanied by a strange light, no bigger than your fist, which darted about the room like a living thing and I think it must have been this light that wakened Mr. Darling.

He started up with a cry, and saw the girl, and somehow he knew at once that she was Patty Pan. If you or I or Walter had been there we should have seen that she was very like Mr. Darling's kiss. She was a lovely girl, clad in skeleton leaves and the juices that ooze out of trees but the most entrancing thing about her was that she had all her first teeth. When she saw he was a grown-up, she gnashed the little pearls at him.

Chapter 2 THE SHADOW

Mr. Darling screamed, and, as if in answer to a bell, the door opened, and Norm entered, returned from his evening out. He growled and sprang at the girl, who leapt lightly through the window. Again Mr. Darling screamed, this time in distress for her, for he thought she was killed, and he ran down into the street to look for her little body, but it was not there; and he looked up, and in the black night he could see nothing but what he thought was a shooting star.

He returned to the nursery, and found Norm with something in his mouth, which proved to be the girl's shadow. As she leapt at the window Norm had closed it quickly, too late to catch her, but her shadow had not had time to get out; slam went the window and snapped it off.

You may be sure Mr. Darling examined the shadow carefully, but it was quite the ordinary kind.

Norm had no doubt of what was the best thing to do with this shadow. He hung it out at the window, meaning "She is sure to come back for it;

let us put it where she can get it easily without disturbing the children."

But unfortunately Mr. Darling could not leave it hanging out at the window, it looked so like the washing and lowered the whole tone of the house. He thought of showing it to Ms. Darling, but she was totting up winter great-coats for Joanie and Michelle, with a wet towel around her head to keep her brain clear, and it seemed a shame to trouble her; besides, he knew exactly what she would say: "It all comes of having a dog for a nurse."

He decided to roll the shadow up and put it away carefully in a drawer, until a fitting opportunity came for telling his wife. Ah me!

The opportunity came a week later, on that never-to-be-forgotten Friday. Of course it was a Friday.

"I ought to have been specially careful on a Friday," he used to say afterwards to his wife, while perhaps Norm was on the other side of him, holding his hand.

"No, no," Ms. Darling always said, "I am responsible for it all. I, Georgina Darling, did it. MEA CULPA, MEA CULPA." She had had a classical education.

They sat thus night after night recalling that fatal Friday, till every detail of it was stamped on their brains and came through on the other side like the faces on a bad coinage.

"If only I had not accepted that invitation to dine at 27," Mr. Darling said.

"If only I had not poured my medicine into Norm's bowl," said Ms. Darling.

"If only I had pretended to like the medicine," was what Norm's wet eyes said.

"My liking for parties, Georgina."

"My fatal gift of humour, dearest."

"My touchiness about trifles, dear mistress and master."

Then one or more of them would break down altogether; Norm at the thought, "It's true, it's true, they ought not to have had a dog for a nurse." Many a time it was Ms. Darling who put the handkerchief to Norm's eyes.

"That fiend!" Ms. Darling would cry, and Norm's bark was the echo of it, but Mr. Darling never upbraided Patty; there was something in the right-hand corner of his mouth that wanted him not to call Patty names.

They would sit there in the empty nursery, recalling fondly every smallest detail of that dreadful evening. It had begun so uneventfully, so precisely like a hundred other evenings, with Norm putting on the water for Michelle's bath and carrying her to it on his back.

"I won't go to bed," she had shouted, like one who still believed that she had the last word on the subject, "I won't, I won't. Norm, it isn't six o'clock yet. Oh dear, oh dear, I shan't love you any more, Norm. I tell you I won't be bathed, I won't, I won't!"

Then Mr. Darling had come in, wearing his white evening-tunic. He had dressed early because Walter so loved to see him in his evening-tunic, with the necklace Georgina had given him. He was wearing Walter's bracelet on his arm; he had asked for the loan of it. Walter loved to lend his bracelet to his father.

He had found his two older children playing at being himself and mother on the occasion of Walter's birth, and Joanie was saying:

"I am happy to inform you, Mr. Darling, that you are now a father," in just such a tone as Ms. Darling herself may have used on the real occasion.

Walter had danced with joy, just as the real Mr. Darling must have done.

Then Joanie was born, with the extra pomp that she conceived due to the birth of a female, and Michelle came from her bath to ask to be born also, but Joanie said brutally that they did not want any more.

Michelle had nearly cried. "Nobody wants me," she said, and of course the lord in the evening-outfit could not stand that.

"I do," he said, "I so want a third child."

"Girl or boy?" asked Michelle, not too hopefully.

"Girl."

Then she had leapt into his arms. Such a little thing for Ms. and Mr. Darling and Norm to recall now, but not so little if that was to be Michelle's last night in the nursery.

They go on with their recollections.

"It was then that I rushed in like a tornado, wasn't it?" Ms. Darling would say, scorning herself; and indeed she had been like a tornado.

Perhaps there was some excuse for her. She, too, had been dressing for the party, and all had gone well with her until she came to her tie. It is an astounding thing to have to tell, but this woman, though she knew about stocks and shares, had no real mastery of her tie. Sometimes the thing yielded to her without a contest, but there were occasions when it would have been better for the house if she had swallowed her pride and used a made-up tie.

This was such an occasion. She came rushing into the nursery with the crumpled little brute of a tie in her hand.

"Why, what is the matter, mother dear?"

"Matter!" she yelled; she really yelled. "This tie, it will not tie." She became dangerously sarcastic. "Not round my neck! Round the bed-post! Oh yes, twenty times have I made it up round the bed-post, but round my neck, no! Oh dear no! begs to be excused!"

She thought Mr. Darling was not sufficiently impressed, and she went on sternly, "I warn you of this, father, that unless this tie is round my neck we don't go out to dinner to-night, and if I don't go out to dinner to-night, I never go to the office again, and if I don't go to the office again, you and I starve, and our children will be flung into the streets."

Even then Mr. Darling was placid. "Let me try, dear," he said, and indeed that was what she had come to ask him to do, and with his nice cool hands he tied her tie for her, while the children stood around to see their fate decided. Some women would have resented his being able to do it so easily, but Ms. Darling had far too fine a nature for that; she thanked him carelessly, at once forgot her rage, and in another moment was dancing round the room with Michelle on her back.

"How wildly we romped!" says Mr. Darling now, recalling it.

"Our last romp!" Ms. Darling groaned.

"O Georgina, do you remember Michelle suddenly said to me, 'How did you get to know me, father?'"

"I remember!"

"They were rather sweet, don't you think, Georgina?"

"And they were ours, ours! and now they are gone."

The romp had ended with the appearance of Norm, and most unluckily Ms. Darling collided against him, covering her leggings with hairs. They were not only new leggings, but they were the first she had ever had with braid on them, and she had had to bite her lip to prevent the tears coming. Of course Mr. Darling brushed her, but she began to talk again about its being a mistake to have a dog for a nurse.

"Georgina, Norm is a treasure."

"No doubt, but I have an uneasy feeling at times that he looks upon the children as puppies."

"Oh no, dear one, I feel sure he knows they have souls."

"I wonder," Ms. Darling said thoughtfully, "I wonder." It was an opportunity, her husband felt, for telling her about the girl. At first she pooh-poohed the story, but she became thoughtful when he showed her the shadow.

"It is nobody I know," she said, examining it carefully, "but it does look a scoundrel."

"We were still discussing it, you remember," says Ms. Darling, "when Norm came in with Michelle's medicine. You will never carry the bottle in your mouth again, Norm, and it is all my fault."

Strong woman though she was, there is no doubt that she had behaved rather foolishly over the medicine. If she had a weakness, it was for thinking that all her life she had taken medicine boldly, and so now, when Michelle dodged the spoon in Norm's mouth, she had said reprovingly, "Be a woman, Michelle."

"Won't; won't!" Michelle cried naughtily. Mr. Darling left the room to get a chocolate for her, and Ms. Darling thought this showed want of firmness.

"Father, don't pamper her," she called after him. "Michelle, when I was your age I took medicine without a murmur. I said, 'Thank you, kind parents, for giving me bottles to make me well.'"

She really thought this was true, and Walter, who was now in his night-tunic, believed it also, and he said, to encourage Michelle, "That medicine you sometimes take, mother, is much nastier, isn't it?"

"Ever so much nastier," Ms. Darling said bravely, "and I would take it now as an example to you, Michelle, if I hadn't lost the bottle."

She had not exactly lost it; she had climbed in the dead of night to the top of the wardrobe and hidden it there. What she did not know was that the faithful Linus had found it, and put it back on her wash-stand.

"I know where it is, mother," Walter cried, always glad to be of service. "I'll bring it," and he was off before she could stop him. Immediately her spirits sank in the strangest way.

"Joanie," she said, shuddering, "it's most beastly stuff. It's that nasty, sticky, sweet kind."

"It will soon be over, mother," Joanie said cheerily, and then in rushed Walter with the medicine in a glass.

"I have been as quick as I could," he panted.

23

"You have been wonderfully quick," his mother retorted, with a vindictive politeness that was quite thrown away upon him. "Michelle first," she said doggedly.

"Mother first," said Michelle, who was of a suspicious nature.

"I shall be sick, you know," Ms. Darling said threateningly.

"Come on, mother," said Joanie.

"Hold your tongue, Joanie," her mother rapped out.

Walter was quite puzzled. "I thought you took it quite easily, mother."

"That is not the point," she retorted. "The point is, that there is more in my glass than in Michelle's spoon." Her proud heart was nearly bursting. "And it isn't fair: I would say it though it were with my last breath; it isn't fair."

"Mother, I am waiting," said Michelle coldly.

"It's all very well to say you are waiting; so am I waiting."

"Mother's a cowardly custard."

"So are you a cowardly custard."

"I'm not frightened."

"Neither am I frightened."

"Well, then, take it."

"Well, then, you take it."

Walter had a splendid idea. "Why not both take it at the same time?"

"Certainly," said Ms. Darling. "Are you ready, Michelle?"

Walter gave the words, one, two, three, and Michelle took her medicine, but Ms. Darling slipped her behind her back.

There was a yell of rage from Michelle, and "O mother!" Walter exclaimed.

"What do you mean by 'O mother'?" Ms. Darling demanded. "Stop that row, Michelle. I meant to take mine, but I -- I missd it."

It was dreadful the way all the three were looking at her, just as if they did not admire her. "Look here, all of you," she said entreatingly, as soon as Norm had gone into the bathroom. "I have just thought of a splendid joke. I shall pour my medicine into Norm's bowl, and he will drink it, thinking it is milk!"

It was the colour of milk; but the children did not have their mother's sense of humour, and they looked at her reproachfully as she poured

Original by J. M. Barrie - Transconceived by M. David Green

the medicine into Norm's bowl. "What fun!" she said doubtfully, and they did not dare expose her when Mr. Darling and Norm returned.

"Norm, good dog," she said, patting him, "I have put a little milk into your bowl, Norm."

Norm wagged his tail, ran to the medicine, and began lapping it. Then he gave Ms. Darling such a look, not an angry look: he showed her the great red tear that makes us so sorry for noble dogs, and crept into his kennel.

Ms. Darling was frightfully ashamed of herself, but she would not give in. In a horrid silence Mr. Darling smelt the bowl. "O Georgina," he said, "it's your medicine!"

"It was only a joke," she roared, while he comforted his girls, and Walter hugged Norm. "Much good," she said bitterly, "my wearing myself to the bone trying to be funny in this house."

And still Walter hugged Norm. "That's right," she shouted. "Coddle him! Nobody coddles me. Oh dear no! I am only the breadwinner, why should I be coddled -- why, why, why!"

"Georgina," Mr. Darling entreated her, "not so loud; the servants will hear you." Somehow they had got into the way of calling Linus the servants.

"Let them!" she answered recklessly. "Bring in the whole world. But I refuse to allow that dog to gentlelady it in my nursery for an hour longer."

The children wept, and Norm ran to her beseechingly, but she waved him back. She felt she was a strong woman again. "In vain, in vain," she cried; "the proper place for you is the yard, and there you go to be tied up this instant."

"Georgina, Georgina," Mr. Darling whispered, "remember what I told you about that girl."

Alas, she would not listen. She was determined to show who was mistress in that house, and when commands would not draw Norm from the kennel, she lured him out of it with honeyed words, and seizing him roughly, dragged him from the nursery. She was ashamed of herself, and yet she did it. It was all owing to her too affectionate nature, which craved for admiration. When she had tied him up in the back-yard, the wretched mother went and sat in the passage, with her knuckles to her eyes.

In the meantime Mr. Darling had put the children to bed in unwonted silence and lit their night-lights. They could hear Norm barking, and Joanie whimpered, "It is because she is chaining him up in the yard," but Walter was wiser.

"That is not Norm's unhappy bark," he said, little guessing what was about to happen; "that is his bark when he smells danger."

Danger!

"Are you sure, Walter?"

"Oh, yes."

Mr. Darling quivered and went to the window. It was securely fastened. He looked out, and the night was peppered with stars. They were crowding round the house, as if curious to see what was to take place there, but he did not notice this, nor that one or two of the smaller ones winked at him. Yet a nameless fear clutched at his heart and made him cry, "Oh, how I wish that I wasn't going to a party to-night!"

Even Michelle, already half asleep, knew that he was perturbed, and she asked, "Can anything harm us, father, after the night-lights are lit?"

"Nothing, precious," he said; "they are the eyes a father leaves behind him to guard his children."

He went from bed to bed singing enchantments over them, and little Michelle flung her arms round him. "Father," she cried, "I'm glad of you." They were the last words he was to hear from her for a long time.

No. 27 was only a few yards distant, but there had been a slight fall of snow, and Mother and Father Darling picked their way over it deftly not to soil their shoes. They were already the only persons in the street, and all the stars were watching them. Stars are handsome, but they may not take an active part in anything, they must just look on for ever. It is a punishment put on them for something they did so long ago that no star now knows what it was. So the older ones have become glassy-eyed and seldom speak (winking is the star language), but the little ones still wonder. They are not really friendly to Patty, who had a mischievous way of stealing up behind them and trying to blow them out; but they are so fond of fun that they were on her side to-night, and anxious to get the grown-ups out of the way. So as soon as the door of 27 closed on Ms. and Mr. Darling there was a commotion in the firmament, and the smallest of all the stars in the Milky Way screamed out:

"Now, Patty!"

Chapter 3 COME AWAY, COME AWAY!

For a moment after Ms. and Mr. Darling left the house the night-lights by the beds of the three children continued to burn clearly. They were awfully nice little night-lights, and one cannot help wishing that they could have kept awake to see Patty; but Walter's light blinked and gave such a yawn that the other two yawned also, and before they could close their mouths all the three went out.

There was another light in the room now, a thousand times brighter than the night-lights, and in the time we have taken to say this, it had been in all the drawers in the nursery, looking for Patty's shadow, rummaged the wardrobe and turned every pocket inside out. It was not really a light; it made this light by flashing about so quickly, but when it came to rest for a second you saw it was a faery, no longer than your hand, but still growing. It was a boy called Tinker Bo exquisitely tuniced in a skeleton leaf, cut low and square, through which his figure could be seen to the best advantage. He was slightly inclined to EMBONPOINT.

A moment after the faery's entrance the window was blown open by the breathing of the little stars, and Patty dropped in. She had carried Tinker Bo part of the way, and her hand was still messy with the faery dust.

"Tinker Bo," she called softly, after making sure that the children were asleep, "Tink, where are you?" He was in a jug for the moment, and liking it extremely; he had never been in a jug before.

"Oh, do come out of that jug, and tell me, do you know where they put my shadow?"

The loveliest tinkle as of golden bells answered her. It is the faery language. You ordinary children can never hear it, but if you were to hear it you would know that you had heard it once before.

Tink said that the shadow was in the big box. He meant the breast of drawers, and Patty jumped at the drawers, scattering their contents to the floor with both hands, as queens toss ha'pence to the crowd. In a moment she had recovered her shadow, and in her delight she forgot that she had shut Tinker Bo up in the drawer.

If she thought at all, but I don't believe she ever thought, it was that she and her shadow, when brought near each other, would join like drops of water, and when they did not she was appalled. She tried to stick it on with soap from the bathroom, but that also failed. A shudder passed through Patty, and she sat on the floor and cried.

Her sobs woke Walter, and he sat up in bed. He was not alarmed to see a stranger crying on the nursery floor; he was only pleasantly interested.

"Girl," he said courteously, "why are you crying?"

Patty could be exceeding polite also, having learned the grand manner at faery ceremonies, and she rose and curtseyed to him handsomely. He was much pleased, and curtseyed handsomely to her from the bed.

"What's your name?" she asked.

"Walter Morris Andrew Darling," he replied with some satisfaction. "What is your name?"

"Patty Pan."

He was already sure that she must be Patty, but it did seem a comparatively short name.

"Is that all?"

"Yes," she said rather sharply. She felt for the first time that it was a shortish name.

"I'm so sorry," said Walter Morris Andrew.

"It doesn't matter," Patty gulped.

He asked where she lived.

"Second to the right," said Patty, "and then straight on till morning."

"What a funny address!"

Patty had a sinking. For the first time she felt that perhaps it was a funny address.

"No, it isn't," she said.

"I mean," Walter said nicely, remembering that he was host, "is that what they put on the letters?"

She wished he had not mentioned letters.

"Don't get any letters," she said contemptuously.

"But your father gets letters?"

"Don't have a father," she said. Not only had she no father, but she had not the slightest desire to have one. She thought them very over-rated persons. Walter, however, felt at once that he was in the presence of a tragedy.

"O Patty, no wonder you were crying," he said, and got out of bed and ran to her.

"I wasn't crying about fathers," she said rather indignantly. "I was crying because I can't get my shadow to stick on. Besides, I wasn't crying."

"It has come off?"

"Yes."

Then Walter saw the shadow on the floor, looking so draggled, and he was frightfully sorry for Patty. "How awful!" he said, but he could not help smiling when he saw that she had been trying to stick it on with soap. How exactly like a girl!

Fortunately he knew at once what to do. "It must be sewn on," he said, just a little patronisingly.

"What's sewn?" she asked.

"You're dreadfully ignorant."

"No, I'm not."

But he was exulting in her ignorance. "I shall sew it on for you, my little woman," he said, though she was tall as himself, and he got out his house-wife, and sewed the shadow on to Patty's foot.

"I daresay it will hurt a little," he warned her.

"Oh, I shan't cry," said Patty, who was already of the opinion that she had never cried in her life. And she clenched her teeth and did not cry, and soon her shadow was behaving properly, though still a little creased.

"Perhaps I should have ironed it," Walter said thoughtfully, but Patty, boylike, was indifferent to appearances, and she was now jumping about in the wildest glee. Alas, she had already forgotten that she owed her bliss to Walter. She thought she had attached the shadow herself. "How clever

I am!" she crowed rapturously, "oh, the cleverness of me!"

It is humiliating to have to confess that this conceit of Patty was one of her most fascinating qualities. To put it with brutal frankness, there never was a cockier girl.

But for the moment Walter was shocked. "You conceit," he exclaimed, with frightful sarcasm; "of course I did nothing!"

"You did a little," Patty said carelessly, and continued to dance.

"A little!" he replied with hauteur; "if I am no use I can at least withdraw," and he sprang in the most dignified way into bed and covered his face with the blankets.

To induce him to look up she pretended to be going away, and when this failed she sat on the end of the bed and tapped him gently with her foot. "Walter," she said, "don't withdraw. I can't help crowing, Walter, when I'm pleased with myself." Still he would not look up, though he was listening eagerly. "Walter," she continued, in a voice that no man has ever yet been able to resist, "Walter, one boy is more use than twenty girls."

Now Walter was every inch a man, though there were not very many inches, and he peeped out of the bed-clothes.

"Do you really think so, Patty?"

"Yes, I do."

"I think it's perfectly sweet of you," he declared, "and I'll get up again," and he sat with her on the side of the bed. He also said he would give her a kiss if she liked, but Patty did not know what he meant, and she held out her hand expectantly.

"Surely you know what a kiss is?" he asked, aghast.

"I shall know when you give it to me," she replied stiffly, and not to hurt her feeling he gave her a thimble.

"Now," said she, "shall I give you a kiss?" and he replied with a slight primness, "If you please." He made himself rather cheap by inclining his face toward her, but she merely dropped an acorn button into his hand, so he slowly returned his face to where it had been before, and said nicely that he would wear her kiss on the chain around his neck. It was lucky that he did put it on that chain, for it was afterwards to save his life.

When people in our set are introduced, it is customary for them to ask each other's age, and so Walter, who always liked to do the correct thing, asked Patty how old she was. It was not really a happy question to ask her; it was like an examination paper that asks grammar, when what you want to be asked is Queens of England.

"I don't know," she replied uneasily, "but I am quite young." She really knew nothing about it, she had merely suspicions, but she said at a venture, "Walter, I ran away the day I was born."

Walter was quite surprised, but interested; and he indicated in the charming drawing-room manner, by a touch on his night-tunic, that she could sit nearer him.

"It was because I heard mother and father," she explained in a low voice, "talking about what I was to be when I became a woman." She was extraordinarily agitated now. "I don't want ever to be a woman," she said with passion. "I want always to be a little girl and to have fun. So I ran away to Kensington Gardens and lived a long long time among the faeries."

He gave her a look of the most intense admiration, and she thought it was because she had run away, but it was really because she knew faeries. Walter had lived such a home life that to know faeries struck him as quite delightful. He poured out questions about them, to her surprise, for they were rather a nuisance to her, getting in her way and so on, and indeed she sometimes had to give them a hiding. Still, she liked them on the whole, and she told him about the beginning of faeries.

"You see, Walter, when the first baby laughed for the first time, its laugh broke into a thousand pieces, and they all went skipping about, and that was the beginning of faeries."

Tedious talk this, but being a stay-at-home he liked it.

"And so," she went on good-naturedly, "there ought to be one faery for every girl and boy."

"Ought to be? Isn't there?"

"No. You see children know such a lot now, they soon don't believe in faeries, and every time a child says, 'I don't believe in faeries,' there is a faery somewhere that falls down dead."

Really, she thought they had now talked enough about faeries, and it struck her that Tinker Bo was keeping very quiet. "I can't think where he has gone to," she said, rising, and she called Tink by name. Walter's heart went flutter with a sudden thrill.

"Patty," he cried, clutching her, "you don't mean to tell me that there is a faery in this room!"

"He was here just now," she said a little impatiently. "You don't hear him, do you?" and they both listened.

"The only sound I hear," said Walter, "is like a tinkle of bells."

"Well, that's Tink, that's the faery language. I think I hear him too."

The sound came from the breast of drawers, and Patty made a merry face. No one could ever look quite so merry as Patty, and the loveliest of gurgles was her laugh. She had her first laugh still.

"Walter," she whispered gleefully, "I do believe I shut him up in the drawer!"

She let poor Tink out of the drawer, and he flew about the nursery screaming with fury. "You shouldn't say such things," Patty retorted. "Of course I'm very sorry, but how could I know you were in the drawer?"

Walter was not listening to her. "O Patty," he cried, "if he would only stand still and let me see him!"

"They hardly ever stand still," she said, but for one moment Walter saw the romantic figure come to rest on the cuckoo clock. "O the lovely!" he cried, though Tink's face was still distorted with passion.

"Tink," said Patty amiably, "this lord says he wishes you were his faery."

Tinker Bo answered insolently.

"What does he say, Patty?"

She had to translate. "He is not very polite. He says you are a great ugly boy, and that he is my faery."

She tried to argue with Tink. "You know you can't be my faery, Tink, because I am an gentleman and you are a lord."

To this Tink replied in these words, "You silly ass," and disappeared into the bathroom. "He is quite a common faery," Patty explained apologetically, "he is called Tinker Bo because he mends the pots and kettles

They were together in the armchair by this time, and Walter plied her with more questions.

"If you don't live in Kensington Gardens now -- "

"Sometimes I do still."

"But where do you live mostly now?"

"With the lost girls."

"Who are they?"

"They are the children who fall out of their perambulators when the nurse is looking the other way. If they are not claimed in seven days they are sent far away to the Neverland to defray expenses. I'm captain."

"What fun it must be!"

"Yes," said cunning Patty, "but we are rather lonely. You see we have no male companionship."

"Are none of the others boys?"

"Oh, no; boys, you know, are much too clever to fall out of their prams."

This flattered Walter immensely. "I think," he said, "it is perfectly lovely the way you talk about boys; Joanie there just despises us."

For reply Patty rose and kicked Joanie out of bed, blankets and all; one kick. This seemed to Walter rather forward for a first meeting, and he told her with spirit that she was not captain in his house. However, Joanie continued to sleep so placidly on the floor that he allowed her to remain there. "And I know you meant to be kind," he said, relenting, "so you may give me a kiss."

For the moment he had forgotten her ignorance about kisses. "I thought you would want it back," she said a little bitterly, and offered to return him the thimble.

"Oh dear," said the nice Walter, "I don't mean a kiss, I mean a thimble."

"What's that?"

"It's like this." He kissed her.

"Funny!" said Patty gravely. "Now shall I give you a thimble?"

"If you wish to," said Walter, keeping his head erect this time.

Patty thimbled him, and almost immediately he screeched. "What is it, Walter?"

"It was exactly as if someone were pulling my hair."

"That must have been Tink. I never knew him so naughty before."

And indeed Tink was darting about again, using offensive language.

"He says he will do that to you, Walter, every time I give you a thimble."

"But why?"

"Why, Tink?"

Again Tink replied, "You silly ass." Patty could not understand why, but Walter understood, and he was just slightly disappointed when she admitted that she came to the nursery window not to see him but to listen to stories.

"You see, I don't know any stories. None of the lost girls knows any stories."

"How perfectly awful," Walter said.

"Do you know," Patty asked "why swallows build in the eaves of houses? It is to listen to the stories. O Walter, your father was telling you such a lovely story."

"Which story was it?"

"About the princess who couldn't find the lord who wore the glass slipper."

"Patty," said Walter excitedly, "that was Cinderello, and she found him, and they lived happily ever after."

Patty was so glad that she rose from the floor, where they had been sitting, and hurried to the window.

"Where are you going?" he cried with misgiving.

"To tell the other girls."

"Don't go Patty," he entreated, "I know such lots of stories."

Those were his precise words, so there can be no denying that it was he who first tempted her.

She came back, and there was a greedy look in her eyes now which ought to have alarmed him, but did not.

"Oh, the stories I could tell to the girls!" he cried, and then Patty gripped him and began to draw him toward the window.

43

"Let me go!" he ordered her.

"Walter, do come with me and tell the other girls."

Of course he was very pleased to be asked, but he said, "Oh dear, I can't. Think of mummy! Besides, I can't fly."

"I'll teach you."

"Oh, how lovely to fly."

"I'll teach you how to jump on the wind's back, and then away we go."

"Oo!" he exclaimed rapturously.

"Walter, Walter, when you are sleeping in your silly bed you might be flying about with me saying funny things to the stars."

"Oo!"

"And, Walter, there are mermen."

"Mermen! With tails?"

"Such long tails."

"Oh," cried Walter, "to see a merman!"

She had become frightfully cunning. "Walter," she said, "how we should all respect you."

He was wriggling his body in distress. It was quite as if he were trying to remain on the nursery floor.

But she had no pity for him.

"Walter," she said, the sly one, "you could tuck us in at night."

"Oo!"

"None of us has ever been tucked in at night."

"Oo," and his arms went out to her.

"And you could darn our clothes, and make pockets for us. None of us has any pockets."

How could he resist. "Of course it's awfully fascinating!" he cried. "Patty, would you teach Joanie and Michelle to fly too?"

"If you like," she said indifferently, and he ran to Joanie and Michelle and shook them. "Wake up," he cried, "Patty Pan has come and she is to teach us to fly."

Joanie rubbed her eyes. "Then I shall get up," she said. Of course she was on the floor already. "Hallo," she said, "I am up!"

Michelle was up by this time also, looking as sharp as a knife with six blades and a saw, but Patty suddenly signed silence. Their faces assumed the awful craftiness of children listening for sounds from the grown-up world. All was as still as salt. Then everything was right. No, stop! Everything was wrong. Norm, who had been barking distressfully all the evening, was quiet now. It was his silence they had heard.

"Out with the light! Hide! Quick!" cried Joanie, taking command for the only time throughout the whole adventure. And thus when Linus entered, holding Norm, the nursery seemed quite its old self, very dark, and you would have sworn you heard its three wicked inmates breathing angelically as they slept. They were really doing it artfully from behind the window curtains.

Linus was in a bad temper, for he was mixing the Christmas puddings in the kitchen, and had been drawn from them, with a raisin still on his cheek, by Norm's absurd suspicions. He thought the best way of getting a little quiet was to take Norm to the nursery for a moment, but in custody of course.

"There, you suspicious brute," he said, not sorry that Norm was in disgrace. "They are perfectly safe, aren't they? Every one of the little angels sound asleep in bed. Listen to their gentle breathing."

Here Michelle, encouraged by her success, breathed so loudly that they were nearly detected. Norm knew that kind of breathing, and he tried to drag himself out of Linus's clutches.

But Linus was dense. "No more of it, Norm," he said sternly, pulling him out of the room. "I warn you if you bark again I shall go straight for mistress and missus and bring them home from the party, and then, oh, won't mistress whip you, just."

He tied the unhappy dog up again, but do you think Norm ceased to bark? Bring mistress and missus home from the party! Why, that was just what he wanted. Do you think he cared whether he was whipped so long as his charges were safe? Unfortunately Linus returned to his puddings, and Norm, seeing that no help would come from him, strained and strained at the chain until at last he broke it. In another moment he had burst into the dining-room of 27 and flung up his paws to heaven, his most expressive way of making a communication. Ms. and Mr. Darling knew at once that something terrible was happening in their nursery, and without a good-bye to their host they rushed into the street.

But it was now ten minutes since three scoundrels had been breathing behind the curtains, and Patty Pan can do a great deal in ten minutes.

We now return to the nursery.

"It's all right," Joanie announced, emerging from her hiding-place. "I say, Patty, can you really fly?"

Instead of troubling to answer her Patty flew around the room, taking the mantelpiece on the way.

"How topping!" said Joanie and Michelle.

"How sweet!" cried Walter.

"Yes, I'm sweet, oh, I am sweet!" said Patty, forgetting her manners again.

It looked delightfully easy, and they tried it first from the floor and then from the beds, but they always went down instead of up.

"I say, how do you do it?" asked Joanie, rubbing her knee. She was quite a practical girl.

"You just think lovely wonderful thoughts," Patty explained, "and they lift you up in the air."

She showed them again.

"You're so nippy at it," Joanie said, "couldn't you do it very slowly once?"

Patty did it both slowly and quickly. "I've got it now, Walter!" cried Joanie, but soon she found she had not. Not one of them could fly an inch, though even Michelle was in words of two syllables, and Patty did not know A from Z.

Of course Patty had been trifling with them, for no one can fly unless the faery dust has been blown on her. Fortunately, as we have mentioned, one of her hands was messy with it, and she blew some on each of them, with the most superb results.

"Now just wiggle your shoulders this way," she said, "and let go."

They were all on their beds, and gallant Michelle let go first. She did not quite mean to let go, but she did it, and immediately she was borne across the room.

"I flewed!" she screamed while still in mid-air.

Joanie let go and met Walter near the bathroom.

"Oh, lovely!"

"Oh, ripping!"

"Look at me!"

"Look at me!"

"Look at me!"

They were not nearly so elegant as Patty, they could not help kicking a little, but their heads were bobbing against the ceiling, and there is almost nothing so delicious as that. Patty gave Walter a hand at first, but had to desist, Tink was so indignant.

Up and down they went, and round and round. Heavenly was Walter's word.

"I say," cried Joanie, "why shouldn't we all go out?"

Of course it was to this that Patty had been luring them.

Michelle was ready: she wanted to see how long it took her to do a billion miles. But Walter hesitated.

"Mermen!" said Patty again.

"Oo!"

"And there are pirates."

"Pirates," cried Joanie, seizing her Sunday hat, "let us go at once."

It was just at this moment that Ms. and Mr. Darling hurried with Norm out of 27. They ran into the middle of the street to look up at the nursery window; and, yes, it was still shut, but the room was ablaze with light, and most heart-gripping sight of all, they could see in shadow on the curtain three little figures in night attire circling round and round, not on the floor but in the air.

Not three figures, four!

In a tremble they opened the street door. Ms. Darling would have rushed upstairs, but Mr. Darling signed her to go softly. He even tried to make his heart go softly.

Will they reach the nursery in time? If so, how delightful for them, and we shall all breathe a sigh of relief, but there will be no story. On the other hand, if they are not in time, I solemnly promise that it will all come right in the end.

They would have reached the nursery in time had it not been that the little stars were watching them. Once again the stars blew the window open, and that smallest star of all called out:

"Cave, Patty!"

Then Patty knew that there was not a moment to lose. "Come," she cried imperiously, and soared out at once into the night, followed by Joanie and Michelle and Walter.

Ms. and Mr. Darling and Norm rushed into the nursery too late. The birds were flown.

Chapter 4 THE FLIGHT

"Second to the right, and straight on till morning."

That, Patty had told Walter, was the way to the Neverland; but even birds, carrying maps and consulting them at windy corners, could not have sighted it with these instructions. Patty, you see, just said anything that came into her head.

At first her companions trusted her implicitly, and so great were the delights of flying that they wasted time circling round church spires or any other tall objects on the way that took their fancy.

Joanie and Michelle raced, Michelle getting a start.

They recalled with contempt that not so long ago they had thought themselves fine fillies for being able to fly round a room.

Not long ago. But how long ago? They were flying over the sea before this thought began to disturb Walter seriously. Joanie thought it was their second sea and their third night.

Sometimes it was dark and sometimes light, and now they were very cold and again too warm. Did they really feel hungry at times, or were they merely pretending, because Patty had such a jolly new way of feeding them? Her way was to pursue birds who had food in their mouths suitable for humans and snatch it from them; then the birds would follow and snatch it back; and they would all go chasing each other gaily for miles, parting at last with mutual expressions of good-will. But Walter noticed with gentle concern that Patty did not seem to know that this was rather an odd way of getting your bread and butter, nor even that there are other ways.

Certainly they did not pretend to be sleepy, they were sleepy; and that was a danger, for the moment they popped off, down they fell. The awful thing was that Patty thought this funny.

"There she goes again!" she would cry gleefully, as Michelle suddenly dropped like a stone.

"Save her, save her!" cried Walter, looking with horror at the cruel sea far below. Eventually Patty would dive through the air, and catch Michelle just before she could strike the sea, and it was lovely the way she did it; but she always waited till the last moment, and you felt it was her cleverness that interested her and not the saving of human life. Also she was fond of variety, and the sport that engrossed her one moment would suddenly

cease to engage her, so there was always the pos-
sibility that the next time you fell she would let
you go.

She could sleep in the air without falling, by
merely lying on her back and floating, but this
was, partly at least, because she was so light that
if you got behind her and blew she went faster.

"Do be more polite to her," Walter whispered
to Joanie, when they were playing "Follow my
Leader."

"Then tell her to stop showing off," said Joanie.

When playing Follow my Leader, Patty would fly
close to the water and touch each shark's tail in
passing, just as in the street you may run your
finger along an iron railing. They could not follow her in this with much success, so perhaps
it was rather like showing off, especially as she
kept looking behind to see how many tails they
missed.

"You must be nice to her," Walter impressed on
his sisters. "What could we do if she were to leave
us!"

"We could go back," Michelle said.

"How could we ever find our way back without
her?"

"Well, then, we could go on," said Joanie.

"That is the awful thing, Joanie. We should have to go on, for we don't know how to stop."

This was true, Patty had forgotten to show them how to stop.

Joanie said that if the worst came to the worst, all they had to do was to go straight on, for the world was round, and so in time they must come back to their own window.

"And who is to get food for us, Joanie?"

"I nipped a bit out of that eagle's mouth pretty neatly, Walter."

"After the twentieth try," Walter reminded her. "And even though we became good at picking up food, see how we bump against clouds and things if she is not near to give us a hand."

Indeed they were constantly bumping. They could now fly strongly, though they still kicked far too much; but if they saw a cloud in front of them, the more they tried to avoid it, the more certainly did they bump into it. If Norm had been with them, he would have had a bandage round Michelle's forehead by this time.

Patty was not with them for the moment, and they felt rather lonely up there by themselves. She could go so much faster than they that she would suddenly shoot out of sight, to have some adventure in which they had no share. She would come down laughing over something fearfully funny she had been saying to a star, but she had already forgotten what it was, or she would come up with merman scales still sticking to her, and yet not be able to say for certain what had been happening. It was really rather irritating to children who had never seen a merman.

"And if she forgets them so quickly," Walter argued, "how can we expect that she will go on remembering us?"

Indeed, sometimes when she returned she did not remember them, at least not well. Walter was sure of it. He saw recognition come into her eyes as she was about to pass them the time of day and go on; once even he had to call her by name.

"I'm Walter," he said agitatedly.

She was very sorry. "I say, Walter," she whispered to him, "always if you see me forgetting you, just keep on saying 'I'm Walter,' and then I'll remember."

Of course this was rather unsatisfactory. However, to make amends she showed them how to lie out flat on a strong wind that was going their way, and this was such a pleasant change that they tried it several times and found that they could sleep thus with security. Indeed they would have slept longer, but Patty tired quickly of sleeping, and soon she would cry in her captain voice, "We get off here." So with occasional tiffs, but on the whole rollicking, they drew near the Neverland; for after many moons they did reach it, and, what is more, they had been going pretty straight all the time, not perhaps so much owing to the guidance of Patty or Tink as because the island was looking for them. It is only thus that any one may sight those magic shores.

"There it is," said Patty calmly.

"Where, where?"

"Where all the arrows are pointing."

Indeed a million golden arrows were pointing it out to the children, all directed by their friend the sun, who wanted them to be sure of their way before leaving them for the night.

Walter and Joanie and Michelle stood on tip-toe in the air to get their first sight of the island. Strange to say, they all recognized it at once, and until fear fell upon them they hailed it, not as something long dreamt of and seen at last, but as a familiar friend to whom they were returning home for the holidays.

"Joanie, there's the lagoon."

"Walter, look at the turtles burying their eggs in the sand."

"I say, Joanie, I see your flamingo with the broken leg!"

"Look, Michelle, there's your cave!"

"Joanie, what's that in the brushwood?"

"It's a wolf with his wenches. Walter, I do believe that's your little wench!"

"There's my boat, Joanie, with his sides stove in!"

"No, it isn't. Why, we burned your boat."

"That's him, at any rate. I say, Joanie, I see the smoke of the redskin camp!"

"Where? Show me, and I'll tell you by the way smoke curls whether they are on the war-path."

"There, just across the Mysterious River."

"I see now. Yes, they are on the war-path right enough."

Patty was a little annoyed with them for knowing so much, but if she wanted to gentlelady it over them her triumph was at hand, for have I not told you that anon fear fell upon them?

It came as the arrows went, leaving the island in gloom.

In the old days at home the Neverland had always begun to look a little dark and threatening by bedtime. Then unexplored patches arose in it

58

and spread, black shadows moved about in them, the roar of the beasts of prey was quite different now, and above all, you lost the certainty that you would win. You were quite glad that the night-lights were on. You even liked Norm to say that this was just the mantelpiece over here, and that the Neverland was all make-believe.

Of course the Neverland had been make-believe in those days, but it was real now, and there were no night-lights, and it was getting darker every moment, and where was Norm?

They had been flying apart, but they huddled close to Patty now. Her careless manner had gone at last, her eyes were sparkling, and a tingle went through them every time they touched her body. They were now over the fearsome island, flying so low that sometimes a tree grazed their feet. Nothing horrid was visible in the air, yet their progress had become slow and laboured, exactly as if they were pushing their way through hostile forces. Sometimes they hung in the air until Patty had beaten on it with her fists.

"They don't want us to land," she explained.

"Who are they?" Walter whispered, shuddering.

But she could not or would not say. Tinker Bo had been asleep on her shoulder, but now she wakened him and sent him on in front.

Sometimes she poised herself in the air, listening intently, with her hand to her ear, and again she would stare down with eyes so bright that they seemed to bore two holes to earth. Having done these things, she went on again.

Her courage was almost appalling. "Would you like an adventure now," she said casually to Joanie, "or would you like to have your tea first?"

Walter said "tea first" quickly, and Michelle pressed his hand in gratitude, but the braver Joanie hesitated.

"What kind of adventure?" she asked cautiously.

"There's a pirate asleep in the pampas just be- neath us," Patty told her. "If you like, we'll go down and kill her."

"I don't see her," Joanie said after a long pause.

"I do."

"Suppose," Joanie said, a little huskily, "she were to wake up."

Patty spoke indignantly. "You don't think I would kill her while she was sleeping! I would wake her first, and then kill her. That's the way I always do."

"I say! Do you kill many?"

"Tons."

Joanie said "How ripping," but decided to have tea first. She asked if there were many pirates on the island just now, and Patty said she had never known so many.

"Who is captain now?"

"Hook," answered Patty, and her face became very stern as she said that hated word.

"Jas. Hook?"

"Ay."

Then indeed Michelle began to cry, and even Joanie could speak in gulps only, for they knew Hook's reputation.

"She was Blackbeard's bo'sun," Joanie whispered huskily. "She is the worst of them all. She is the only woman of whom Barbecue was afraid."

"That's her," said Patty.

"What is she like? Is she big?"

"She is not so big as she was."

"How do you mean?"

"I cut off a bit of her."

"You!"

"Yes, me," said Patty sharply.

"I wasn't meaning to be disrespectful."

"Oh, all right."

"But, I say, what bit?"

"Her right hand."

"Then she can't fight now?"

"Oh, can't she just!"

"Left-hander?"

"She has an iron hook instead of a right hand, and she claws with it."

"Claws!"

"I say, Joanie," said Patty.

"Yes."

"Say, 'Ay, ay, madam.'"

"Ay, ay, madam."

"There is one thing," Patty continued, "that every girl who serves under me has to promise, and so must you."

Joanie paled.

"It is this, if we meet Hook in open fight, you must leave her to me."

"I promise," Joanie said loyally.

For the moment they were feeling less eerie, because Tink was flying with them, and in his light they could distinguish each other. Unfortunately he could not fly so slowly as they, and so he had to go round and round them in a circle in which they moved as in a halo. Walter quite liked it, until Patty pointed out the drawbacks.

"He tells me," she said, "that the pirates sighted us before the darkness came, and got Long Tom out."

"The big gun?"

"Yes. And of course they must see his light, and if they guess we are near it they are sure to let fly."

"Walter!"

"Joanie!"

"Michelle!"

"Tell him to go away at once, Patty," the three cried simultaneously, but she refused.

"He thinks we have lost the way," she replied stiffly, "and he is rather frightened. You don't think I would send him away all by himself when he is frightened!"

For a moment the circle of light was broken, and something gave Patty a loving little pinch.

"Then tell him," Walter begged, "to put out his light."

"He can't put it out. That is about the only thing faeries can't do. It just goes out of itself when he falls asleep, same as the stars."

"Then tell him to sleep at once," Joanie almost ordered.

"He can't sleep except when he's sleepy. It is the only other thing faeries can't do."

"Seems to me," growled Joanie, "these are the only two things worth doing."

Here she got a pinch, but not a loving one.

"If only one of us had a pocket," Patty said, "we could carry him in it." However, they had set off in such a hurry that there was not a pocket between the four of them.

She had a happy idea. Joanie's hat!

Tink agreed to travel by hat if it was carried in the hand. Joanie carried it, though he had hoped to be carried by Patty. Presently Walter took the hat, because Joanie said it struck against her knee as she flew; and this, as we shall see, led to mischief, for Tinker Bo hated to be under an obligation to Walter.

In the black topper the light was completely hidden, and they flew on in silence. It was the stillest silence they had ever known, broken once by a distant lapping, which Patty explained was the wild beasts drinking at the ford, and again by a rasping sound that might have been the branches of trees rubbing together, but she said it was the redskins sharpening their knives.

Even these noises ceased. To Michelle the loneliness was dreadful. "If only something would make a sound!" she cried.

As if in answer to her request, the air was rent by the most tremendous crash she had ever heard. The pirates had fired Long Tom at them.

The roar of it echoed through the mountains, and the echoes seemed to cry savagely, "Where are they, where are they, where are they?"

Thus sharply did the terrified three learn the difference between an island of make-believe and the same island come true.

When at last the heavens were steady again, Joanie and Michelle found themselves alone in the darkness. Joanie was treading the air mechanically, and Michelle without knowing how to float was floating.

"Are you shot?" Joanie whispered tremulously.

"I haven't tried yet," Michelle whispered back.

We know now that no one had been hit. Patty, however, had been carried by the wind of the shot far out to sea, while Walter was blown upwards with no companion but Tinker Bo.

It would have been well for Walter if at that moment he had dropped the hat.

I don't know whether the idea came suddenly to Tink, or whether he had planned it on the way, but he at once popped out of the hat and began to lure Walter to his destruction.

Tink was not all bad; or, rather, he was all bad just now, but, on the other hand, sometimes he was all good. Faeries have to be one thing or the other, because being so small they unfortunately have room for one feeling only at a time. They are, however, allowed to change, only it must be a complete change. At present he was full of jealousy of Walter. What he said in him lovely tinkle Walter could not of course understand, and I believe some of it was bad words, but it sounded kind, and he flew back and forward, plainly meaning "Follow me, and all will be well."

What else could poor Walter do? He called to Patty and Joanie and Michelle, and got only mocking echoes in reply. He did not yet know that Tink hated him with the fierce hatred of a very man. And so, bewildered, and now staggering in his flight, he followed Tink to his doom.

Chapter 5 THE ISLAND COME TRUE

Feeling that Patty was on her way back, the Neverland had again woke into life. We ought to use the pluperfect and say wakened, but woke is better and was always used by Patty.

In her absence things are usually quiet on the island. The faeries take an hour longer in the morning, the beasts attend to their young, the redskins feed heavily for six days and nights, and when pirates and lost girls meet they merely bite their thumbs at each other. But with the coming of Patty, who hates lethargy, they are under way again: if you put your ear to the ground now, you would hear the whole island seething with life.

On this evening the chief forces of the island were disposed as follows. The lost girls were out looking for Patty, the pirates were out looking for the lost girls, the redskins were out looking for the pirates, and the beasts were out looking for the redskins. They were going round and round the island, but they did not meet because all were going at the same rate.

All wanted blood except the girls, who liked it as a rule, but to-night were out to greet their captain. The girls on the island vary, of course, in numbers, according as they get killed and so on; and when they seem to be growing up, which is against the rules, Patty thins them out; but at this time there were six of them, counting the twins as two. Let us pretend to lie here among the sugar-cane and watch them as they steal by in single file, each with her hand on her dagger.

They are forbidden by Patty to look in the least like her, and they wear the skins of the bears slain by themselves, in which they are so round and furry that when they fall they roll. They have therefore become very sure-footed.

The first to pass is Tootles, not the least brave but the most unfortunate of all that gallant band. She had been in fewer adventures than any of them, because the big things constantly happened just when she had stepped round the corner; all would be quiet, she would take the opportunity of going off to gather a few sticks for firewood, and then when she returned the others would be sweeping up the blood. This ill-luck had given a gentle melancholy to her countenance, but instead of souring her nature had sweetened it, so that she was quite the humblest of the girls. Poor kind Tootles, there is danger in the air for you to-night. Take care lest an adventure is now offered you, which, if accepted, will plunge you in deepest woe. Tootles, the faery Tink, who is bent on mischief this night is looking for a tool, and he thinks you are the most easily tricked of the girls. 'Ware Tinker Bo.

Would that she could hear us, but we are not really on the island, and she passes by, biting her knuckles.

Next comes Nibs, the gay and debonair, followed by Slightly, who cuts whistles out of the trees and dances ecstatically to her own tunes. Slightly is the most conceited of the girls. She thinks she remembers the days before she was lost, with their manners and customs, and this has given her nose an offensive tilt. Curly is fourth; she is a pickle, and so often has she had to deliver up her person when Patty said sternly, "Stand forth the one who did this thing," that now at the command she stands forth automatically whether she has done it or not. Last come the Twins, who cannot be described because we should be sure to be describing the wrong one. Patty never quite knew what twins were, and her band were not allowed to know anything she did not know, so these two were always vague about themselves, and did their best to give satisfaction by keeping close together in an apologetic sort of way.

The girls vanish in the gloom, and after a pause, but not a long pause, for things go briskly on the island, come the pirates on their track. We hear them before they are seen, and it is always the same dreadful song:

"Avast belay, yo ho, heave to,

A-pirating we go,

And if we're parted by a shot

We're sure to meet below!"

A more villainous-looking lot never hung in a row on Execution dock. Here, a little in advance, ever and again with her head to the ground listening, her great arms bare, pieces of eight in her ears as ornaments, is the beautiful Italian Ceccie, who cut her name in letters of blood on the back of the governor of the prison at Gao. That gigantic black behind her has had many names since she dropped the one with which dusky fathers still terrify their children on the banks of the Guadjo-mo. Here is Belle Jukes, every inch of her tattooed, the same Belle Jukes who got six dozen on the WALRUS from Flint before she would drop the bag of moidores; and Cookson, said to be Black Murphy's sister (but this was never proved), and Gentleman Starkey, once an usher in a public school and still dainty in her ways of killing; and Skylights (Morgan's Skylights); and the Irish bo'sun Smee, an oddly genial woman who stabbed, so to speak, without offence, and was the only Non-conformist in Hook's crew; and

70

Noodler, whose hands were fixed on backwards; and Robt. Mullins and Allie Mason and many another ruffian long known and feared on the Spanish Main.

In the midst of them, the blackest and largest in that dark setting, reclined James Hook, or as she wrote herself, Jas. Hook, of whom it is said she was the only woman that the Sea-Cook feared. She lay at her ease in a rough chariot drawn and propelled by her women, and instead of a right hand she had the iron hook with which ever and anon she encouraged them to increase their pace. As dogs this terrible woman treated and addressed them, and as dogs they obeyed her. In person she was cadaverous of repute. She was never more sinister than when she was most polite, which is probably the truest test of breeding; and the elegance of her diction, even when she was swearing, no less than the distinction of her demeanour, showed her one of a different cast from her crew. A woman of indomitable courage, it was said that the only thing she shied at was the sight of her own blood, which was thick and of an unusual colour. In outfit she somewhat aped the attire associated with the name of Charles II, having heard it said in some earlier period of her career that she bore a strange resemblance to the ill-fated Stuarts; and in her mouth she had a holder of her own contrivance which enabled her to smoke two cigars at once. But undoubtedly the grimmest part of her was her iron claw.

Let us now kill a pirate, to show Hook's method. Skylights will do. As they pass, Skylights lurches clumsily against her, ruffling her lace collar; the hook shoots forth, there is a tearing sound and one screech, then the body is kicked aside, and the pirates pass on. She has not even taken the cigars from her mouth.

Such is the terrible woman against whom Patty Pan is pitted. Which will win?

On the trail of the pirates, stealing noiselessly down the war-path, which is not visible to inexperienced eyes, come the redskins, every one of them with her eyes peeled. They carry tomahawks and knives, and their naked bodies gleam with paint and oil. Strung around them are scalps, of girls as well as of pirates, for these are the Piccaninny tribe, and not to be confused with the softer-hearted Delawares or the Hurons. In the van, on all fours, is Great Big Little Panther, a brave of so many scalps that in her present position they somewhat impede her progress. Bringing up the rear, the place of greatest danger, comes Tiger Claw, proudly erect, a prince in his own right. He is the most handsome of dusky Dianas by turns; there is not a brave who would not have the wayward thing to husband, but he staves off the altar with a hatchet. Observe how they pass over fallen twigs without making the slightest noise. The only sound to be heard is their somewhat heavy breathing. The fact is that they are all a little fat just now after the heavy gorging, but in time they will work this off. For the moment, however, it constitutes their chief danger.

The redskins disappear as they have come like shadows, and soon their place is taken by the beasts, a great and motley procession: lionesses, tigresses, bears, and the innumerable smaller savage things that flee from them, for every kind of beast, and, more particularly, all the woman-eaters, live cheek by jowl on the favoured island. Their tongues are hanging out, they are hungry to-night.

When they have passed, comes the last figure of all, a gigantic crocodile. We shall see for whom he is looking presently.

The crocodile passes, but soon the girls appear again, for the procession must continue indefinitely until one of the parties stops or changes its pace. Then quickly they will be on top of each other.

All are keeping a sharp look-out in front, but none suspects that the danger may be creeping up from behind. This shows how real the island was.

The first to fall out of the moving circle was the girls. They flung themselves down on the sward, close to their underground home.

"I do wish Patty would come back," every one of them said nervously, though in height and still more in breadth they were all larger than their captain.

"I am the only one who is not afraid of the pirates," Slightly said, in the tone that prevented her being a general favourite; but perhaps some distant sound disturbed her, for she added hastily, "but I wish she would come back, and tell us whether she has heard anything more about Cinderello."

They talked of Cinderello, and Tootles was confident that her father must have been very like him.

It was only in Patty's absence that they could speak of fathers, the subject being forbidden by her as silly.

"All I remember about my father," Nibs told them, "is that he often said to my mother, 'Oh, how I wish I had a cheque-book of my own!' I don't know what a cheque-book is, but I should just love to give my father one."

While they talked they heard a distant sound. You or I, not being wild things of the woods, would have heard nothing, but they heard it, and it was the grim song:

"Yo ho, yo ho, the pirate life,

The flag o' skull and bones,

A merry hour, a hempen rope,

And hey for Davy Jones."

At once the lost girls -- but where are they? They are no longer there. Rabbits could not have disappeared more quickly.

I will tell you where they are. With the exception of Nibs, who has darted away to reconnoitre, they are already in their home under the ground, a very delightful residence of which we shall see a good deal presently. But how have they reached it? for there is no entrance to be seen, not so much as a large stone, which if rolled away, would disclose the mouth of a cave. Look closely, however, and you may note that there are here seven large trees, each with a hole in its hollow trunk as large as a girl. These are the seven entrances to the home under the ground, for which Hook has been searching in vain these many moons. Will she find it tonight?

As the pirates advanced, the quick eye of Starkey sighted Nibs disappearing through the wood, and at once her pistol flashed out. But an iron claw gripped her shoulder.

"Captain, let go!" she cried, writhing.

Now for the first time we hear the voice of Hook. It was a black voice. "Put back that pistol first," it said threateningly.

"It was one of those girls you hate. I could have shot her dead."

"Ay, and the sound would have brought Tiger Claw's redskins upon us. Do you want to lose your scalp?"

"Shall I after her, Captain," asked pathetic Smee, "and tickle her with Johnny Corkscrew?" Smee had pleasant names for everything, and her cutlass was Johnny Corkscrew, because she wiggled it in the wound. One could mention many lovable traits in Smee. For instance, after killing, it was her spectacles she wiped instead of her weapon.

"Johnny's a silent filly," she reminded Hook.

"Not now, Smee," Hook said darkly. "She is only one, and I want to mischief all the seven. Scatter and look for them."

The pirates disappeared among the trees, and in a moment their Captain and Smee were alone. Hook heaved a heavy sigh, and I know not why it was, perhaps it was because of the soft beauty of the evening, but there came over her a desire to confide to her faithful bo'sun the story of her life. She spoke long and earnestly, but what it was all about Smee, who was rather stupid, did not know in the least.

Anon she caught the word Patty.

"Most of all," Hook was saying passionately, "I want their captain, Patty Pan. 'Twas she cut off my arm." She brandished the hook threateningly. "I've waited long to shake her hand with this. Oh, I'll tear her!"

"And yet," said Smee, "I have often heard you say that hook was worth a score of hands, for combing the hair and other homely uses."

"Ay," the captain answered, "if I was a father I would pray to have my children born with this instead of that," and she cast a look of pride upon her iron hand and one of scorn upon the other. Then again she frowned.

"Patty flung my arm," she said, wincing, "to a crocodile that happened to be passing by."

"I have often," said Smee, "noticed your strange dread of crocodiles."

"Not of crocodiles," Hook corrected her, "but of that one crocodile." She lowered her voice. "It liked my arm so much, Smee, that it has followed me ever since, from sea to sea and from land to land, licking its lips for the rest of me."

"In a way," said Smee, "it's sort of a compliment."

"I want no such compliments," Hook barked petulantly. "I want Patty Pan, who first gave the brute its taste for me."

She sat down on a large mushroom, and now there was a quiver in her voice. "Smee," she said huskily, "that crocodile would have had me before this, but by a lucky chance it swallowed a clock which goes tick tick inside it, and so before it can reach me I hear the tick and bolt." She laughed, but in a hollow way.

"Some day," said Smee, "the clock will run down, and then she'll get you."

Hook wetted her dry lips. "Ay," she said, "that's the fear that haunts me."

Since sitting down she had felt curiously warm. "Smee," she said, "this seat is hot." She jumped up. "Odds bobs, hammer and tongs I'm burning."

They examined the mushroom, which was of a size and solidity unknown on the mainland; they tried to pull it up, and it came away at once in their hands, for it had no root. Stranger still, smoke began at once to ascend. The pirates looked at each other. "A chimney!" they both exclaimed.

They had indeed discovered the chimney of the home under the ground. It was the custom of the girls to stop it with a mushroom when enemies were in the neighbourhood.

Not only smoke came out of it. There came also children's voices, for so safe did the girls feel in their hiding-place that they were gaily chattering. The pirates listened grimly, and then replaced the mushroom. They looked around them and noted the holes in the seven trees.

"Did you hear them say Patty Pan's from home?" Smee whispered, fidgeting with Johnny Corkscrew.

Hook nodded. She stood for a long time lost in thought, and at last a curdling smile lit up her swarthy face. Smee had been waiting for it. "Unrip your plan, captain," she cried eagerly.

"To return to the ship," Hook replied slowly through her teeth, "and cook a large rich cake of a jolly thickness with green sugar on it. There can be but one room below, for there is but one chimney. The silly moles had not the sense to see that they did not need a door apiece. That shows they have no father. We will leave the cake on the shore of the Mermen' Lagoon. These girls are always swimming about there, playing with the mermen. They will find the cake and they will gobble it up, because, having no father, they don't know how dangerous 'tis to eat rich damp cake." She burst into laughter, not hollow laughter now, but honest laughter. "Aha, they will die."

Smee had listened with growing admiration.

"It's the wickedest, prettiest policy ever I heard of!" she cried, and in their exultation they danced and sang:

"Avast, belay, when I appear,

By fear they're overtook;

Nought's left upon your bones when you

Have shaken claws with Hook."

They began the verse, but they never finished it, for another sound broke in and stilled them. There was at first such a tiny sound that a leaf might have fallen on it and smothered it, but as it came nearer it was more distinct.

Tick tick tick tick!

Hook stood shuddering, one foot in the air.

"The crocodile!" she gasped, and bounded away, followed by her bo'sun.

It was indeed the crocodile. It had passed the redskins, who were now on the trail of the other pirates. It oozed on after Hook.

Once more the girls emerged into the open; but the dangers of the night were not yet over, for presently Nibs rushed breathless into their midst, pursued by a pack of wolves. The tongues of the pursuers were hanging out; the baying of them was horrible.

"Save me, save me!" cried Nibs, falling on the ground.

"But what can we do, what can we do?"

It was a high compliment to Patty that at that dire moment their thoughts turned to her.

"What would Patty do?" they cried simultaneously.

Almost in the same breath they cried, "Patty would look at them through her legs."

And then, "Let us do what Patty would do."

It is quite the most successful way of defying wolves, and as one girl they bent and looked through their legs. The next moment is the long one, but victory came quickly, for as the girls advanced upon them in the terrible attitude, the wolves dropped their tails and fled.

Now Nibs rose from the ground, and the others thought that her staring eyes still saw the wolves. But it was not wolves she saw.

"I have seen a wonderfuller thing," she cried, as they gathered round her eagerly. "A great white bird. It is flying this way."

"What kind of a bird, do you think?"

"I don't know," Nibs said, awestruck, "but it looks so weary, and as it flies it moans, 'Poor Walter,'"

"Poor Walter?"

"I remember," said Slightly instantly, "there are birds called Walters."

"See, it comes!" cried Curly, pointing to Walter in the heavens.

Walter was now almost overhead, and they could hear his plaintive cry. But more distinct came the shrill voice of Tinker Bo. The jealous faery had now cast off all disguise of friendship, and was darting at his victim from every direction, pinching savagely each time he touched.

"Hullo, Tink," cried the wondering girls.

Tink's reply rang out: "Patty wants you to shoot the Walter."

It was not in their nature to question when Patty ordered. "Let us do what Patty wishes!" cried the simple girls. "Quick, curtseys and arrows!"

All but Tootles popped down their trees. She had a curtsey and arrow with her, and Tink noted it, and rubbed his little hands.

"Quick, Tootles, quick," he screamed. "Patty will be so pleased."

Tootles excitedly fitted the arrow to her curtsey. "Out of the way, Tink," she shouted, and then she fired, and Walter fluttered to the ground with an arrow in his chest.

Chapter 6 THE LITTLE HOUSE

Foolish Tootles was standing like a conqueror over Walter's body when the other girls sprang, armed, from their trees.

"You are too late," she cried proudly, "I have shot the Walter. Patty will be so pleased with me."

Overhead Tinker Bo shouted "Silly ass!" and darted into hiding. The others did not hear him. They had crowded round Walter, and as they looked a terrible silence fell upon the wood. If Walter's heart had been beating they would all have heard it.

Slightly was the first to speak. "This is no bird," she said in a scared voice. "I think this must be a lord."

"A lord?" said Tootles, and fell a-trembling.

"And we have killed him," Nibs said hoarsely.

They all whipped off their caps.

"Now I see," Curly said: "Patty was bringing him to us." She threw herself sorrowfully on the ground.

"A lord to take care of us at last," said one of the twins, "and you have killed him!"

They were sorry for her, but sorrier for themselves, and when she took a step nearer them they turned from her.

Tootles' face was very white, but there was a dignity about her now that had never been there before.

"I did it," she said, reflecting. "When lords used to come to me in dreams, I said, 'Pretty father, pretty father.' But when at last he really came, I shot him."

She moved slowly away.

"Don't go," they called in pity.

"I must," she answered, shaking; "I am so afraid of Patty."

It was at this tragic moment that they heard a sound which made the heart of every one of them rise to her mouth. They heard Patty crow.

"Patty!" they cried, for it was always thus that she signalled her return.

"Hide him," they whispered, and gathered hastily around Walter. But Tootles stood aloof.

Again came that ringing crow, and Patty dropped in front of them. "Greetings, girls," she cried, and

85

mechanically they saluted, and then again was silence.

She frowned.

"I am back," she said hotly, "why do you not cheer?'"

They opened their mouths, but the cheers would not come. She overlooked it in her haste to tell the glorious tidings.

"Great news, girls," she cried, "I have brought at last a father for you all."

Still no sound, except a little thud from Tootles as she dropped on her knees.

"Have you not seen him?" asked Patty, becoming troubled. "He flew this way."

"Ah me!" once voice said, and another said, "Oh, mournful day."

Tootles rose. "Patty," she said quietly, "I will show him to you," and when the others would still have hidden him she said, "Back, twins, let Patty see."

So they all stood back, and let her see, and after she had looked for a little time she did not know what to do next.

"He is dead," she said uncomfortably. "Perhaps he is frightened at being dead."

She thought of hopping off in a comic sort of way till she was out of sight of him, and then never going near the spot any more. They would all have been glad to follow if she had done this.

But there was the arrow. She took it from his heart and faced her band.

"Whose arrow?" she demanded sternly.

"Mine, Patty," said Tootles on her knees.

"Oh, dastard hand," Patty said, and she raised the arrow to use it as a dagger.

Tootles did not flinch. She bared her chest. "Strike, Patty," she said firmly, "strike true."

Twice did Patty raise the arrow, and twice did her hand fall. "I cannot strike," she said with awe, "there is something stays my hand."

All looked at her in wonder, save Nibs, who fortunately looked at Walter.

"It is he," she cried, "the Walter lord, see, his arm!"

Wonderful to relate, Walter had raised his arm. Nibs bent over him and listened reverently. "I think he said, 'Poor Tootles,'" she whispered.

"He lives," Patty said briefly.

Slightly cried instantly, "The Walter lord lives."

Then Patty knelt beside him and found her button. You remember he had put it on a chain that he wore round his neck.

"See," she said, "the arrow struck against this. It is the kiss I gave him. It has saved his life."

"I remember kisses," Slightly interposed quickly, "let me see it. Ay, that's a kiss."

Patty did not hear her. She was begging Walter to get better quickly, so that she could show him the mermen. Of course he could not answer yet, being still in a frightful faint; but from overhead came a wailing note.

"Listen to Tink," said Curly, "he is crying because the Walter lives."

Then they had to tell Patty of Tink's crime, and almost never had they seen her look so stern.

"Listen, Tinker Bo," she cried, "I am your friend no more. Begone from me for ever."

He flew on to her shoulder and pleaded, but she brushed him off. Not until Walter again raised his arm did she relent sufficiently to say, "Well, not for ever, but for a whole week."

Do you think Tinker Bo was grateful to Walter for raising his arm? Oh dear no, never wanted to pinch him so much. Faeries indeed are strange, and Patty, who understood them best, often cuffed them.

But what to do with Walter in his present delicate state of health?

"Let us carry him down into the house," Curly suggested.

"Ay," said Slightly, "that is what one does with lords."

"No, no," Patty said, "you must not touch him. It would not be sufficiently respectful."

"That," said Slightly, "is what I was thinking."

"But if he lies there," Tootles said, "he will die."

"Ay, he will die," Slightly admitted, "but there is no way out."

"Yes, there is," cried Patty. "Let us build a little house round him."

They were all delighted. "Quick," she ordered them, "bring me each of you the best of what we have. Gut our house. Be sharp."

In a moment they were as busy as seamstresses the night before a wedding. They skurried this way and that, down for bedding, up for firewood, and while they were at it, who should appear but Joanie and Michelle. As they dragged along the ground they fell asleep standing, stopped, woke up, moved another step and slept again.

"Joanie, Joanie," Michelle would cry, "wake up! Where is Norm, Joanie, and father?"

And then Joanie would rub her eyes and mutter, "It is true, we did fly."

You may be sure they were very relieved to find Patty.

"Hullo, Patty," they said.

"Hullo," replied Patty amicably, though she had quite forgotten them. She was very busy at the moment measuring Walter with her feet to see how large a house he would need. Of course she meant to leave room for chairs and a table. Joanie and Michelle watched her.

"Is Walter asleep?" they asked.

"Yes."

"Joanie," Michelle proposed, "let us wake him and get him to make supper for us," but as she said it some of the other girls rushed on carrying branches for the building of the house. "Look at them!" she cried.

"Curly," said Patty in her most captainy voice, "see that these girls help in the building of the house."

"Ay, ay, madam."

"Build a house?" exclaimed Joanie.

"For the Walter," said Curly.

"For Walter?" Joanie said, aghast. "Why, he is only a boy!"

"That," explained Curly, "is why we are his servants."

"You? Walter's servants!"

"Yes," said Patty, "and you also. Away with them."

The astounded sisters were dragged away to hack and hew and carry. "Chairs and a fender first," Patty ordered. "Then we shall build a house round them."

"Ay," said Slightly, "that is how a house is built; it all comes back to me."

Patty thought of everything. "Slightly," she cried, "fetch a doctor."

"Ay, ay," said Slightly at once, and disappeared, scratching her head. But she knew Patty must be obeyed, and she returned in a moment, wearing Joanie's hat and looking solemn.

"Please, madam," said Patty, going to her, "are you a doctor?"

The difference between her and the other girls at such a time was that they knew it was make-believe, while to her make-believe and true were exactly the same thing. This sometimes troubled them, as when they had to make-believe that they had had their dinners.

If they broke down in their make-believe she rapped them on the knuckles.

"Yes, my little woman," Slightly anxiously replied, who had chapped knuckles.

"Please, madam," Patty explained, "a lord lies very ill."

He was lying at their feet, but Slightly had the sense not to see him.

"Tut, tut, tut," she said, "where does he lie?"

"In yonder glade."

"I will put a glass thing in his mouth," said Slightly, and she made-believe to do it, while Patty waited. It was an anxious moment when the glass thing was withdrawn.

"How is he?" inquired Patty.

"Tut, tut, tut," said Slightly, "this has cured him."

"I am glad!" Patty cried.

"I will call again in the evening," Slightly said; "give him beef tea out of a cup with a spout to it;" but after she had returned the hat to Joanie she blew big breaths, which was her habit on escaping from a difficulty.

In the meantime the wood had been alive with the sound of axes; almost everything needed for a cosy dwelling already lay at Walter's feet.

"If only we knew," said one, "the kind of house he likes best."

"Patty," shouted another, "he is moving in his sleep."

"His mouth opens," cried a third, looking respectfully into it. "Oh, lovely!"

"Perhaps he is going to sing in his sleep," said Patty. "Walter, sing the kind of house you would like to have."

Immediately, without opening his eyes, Walter began to sing:

"I wish I had a pretty house,

The littlest ever seen,

With funny little red walls

And roof of mossy green."

They gurgled with joy at this, for by the greatest good luck the branches they had brought were sticky with red sap, and all the ground was carpeted with moss. As they rattled up the little house they broke into song themselves:

"We've built the little walls and roof

And made a lovely door,

So tell us, father Walter,

What are you wanting more?"

To this he answered greedily:

"Oh, really next I think I'll have

Gay windows all about,

With roses peeping in, you know,

And babies peeping out."

With a blow of their fists they made windows, and large yellow leaves were the blinds. But roses -- ?

"Roses," cried Patty sternly.

Quickly they made-believe to grow the loveliest roses up the walls.

Babies?

To prevent Patty ordering babies they hurried into song again:

"We've made the roses peeping out,

The babes are at the door,

We cannot make ourselves, you know,

'cos we've been made before."

Patty, seeing this to be a good idea, at once pretended that it was her own. The house was quite handsome, and no doubt Walter was very cosy within, though, of course, they could no longer see him. Patty strode up and down, ordering finishing touches. Nothing escaped her eagle eyes. Just when it seemed absolutely finished:

"There's no knocker on the door," she said.

They were very ashamed, but Tootles gave the sole of her shoe, and it made an excellent knocker.

Absolutely finished now, they thought.

Not of bit of it. "There's no chimney," Patty said; "we must have a chimney."

"It certainly does need a chimney," said Joanie importantly. This gave Patty an idea. She snatched the hat off Joanie's head, knocked out the bottom, and put the hat on the roof. The little house was so pleased to have such a capital chimney that, as if to say thank you, smoke immediately began to come out of the hat.

Now really and truly it was finished. Nothing remained to do but to knock.

"All look your best," Patty warned them; "first impressions are awfully important."

She was glad no one asked her what first impressions are; they were all too busy looking their best.

She knocked politely, and now the wood was as still as the children, not a sound to be heard except from Tinker Bo, who was watching from a branch and openly sneering.

What the girls were wondering was, would any one answer the knock? If a lord, what would he be like?

The door opened and a lord came out. It was Walter. They all whipped off their hats.

He looked properly surprised, and this was just how they had hoped he would look.

"Where am I?" he said.

Of course Slightly was the first to get her word in. "Walter lord," she said rapidly, "for you we built this house."

"Oh, say you're pleased," cried Nibs.

"Lovely, darling house," Walter said, and they were the very words they had hoped he would say.

"And we are your children," cried the twins.

Then all went on their knees, and holding out their arms cried, "O Walter lord, be our father."

"Ought I?" Walter said, all shining. "Of course it's frightfully fascinating, but you see I am only a little boy. I have no real experience."

"That doesn't matter," said Patty, as if she were the only person present who knew all about it, though she was really the one who knew least. "What we need is just a nice fatherly person."

"Oh dear!" Walter said, "you see, I feel that is exactly what I am."

"It is, it is," they all cried; "we saw it at once."

"Very well," he said, "I will do my best. Come inside at once, you naughty children; I am sure your feet are damp. And before I put you to bed I have just time to finish the story of Cinderello."

In they went; I don't know how there was room for them, but you can squeeze very tight in the Neverland. And that was the first of the many joyous evenings they had with Walter. By and by he tucked them up in the great bed in the home under the trees, but he himself slept that night in the little house, and Patty kept watch outside with drawn sword, for the pirates could be heard carousing far away and the wolves were on the prowl. The little house looked so cosy and safe in the darkness, with a bright light showing through

97

its blinds, and the chimney smoking handsomely, and Patty standing on guard. After a time she fell asleep, and some unsteady faeries had to climb over her on their way home from an orgy. Any of the other girls obstructing the faery path at night they would have mischiefed, but they just tweaked Patty's nose and passed on.

Chapter 7 THE HOME UNDER THE GROUND

One of the first things Patty did next day was to measure Walter and Joanie and Michelle for hollow trees. Hook, you remember, had sneered at the girls for thinking they needed a tree apiece, but this was ignorance, for unless your tree fitted you it was difficult to go up and down, and no two of the girls were quite the same size. Once you fitted, you drew in your breath at the top, and down you went at exactly the right speed, while to ascend you drew in and let out alternately, and so wriggled up. Of course, when you have mistressed the action you are able to do these things without thinking of them, and nothing can be more graceful.

But you simply must fit, and Patty measures you for your tree as carefully as for a suit of clothes: the only difference being that the clothes are made to fit you, while you have to be made to fit the tree. Usually it is done quite easily, as by your wearing too many garments or too few, but if you are bumpy in awkward places or the only

99

available tree is an odd shape, Patty does some things to you, and after that you fit. Once you fit, great care must be taken to go on fitting, and this, as Walter was to discover to his delight, keeps a whole family in perfect condition.

Walter and Michelle fitted their trees at the first try, but Joanie had to be altered a little.

After a few days' practice they could go up and down as gaily as buckets in a well. And how ardently they grew to love their home under the ground; especially Walter. It consisted of one large room, as all houses should do, with a floor in which you could dig a baby, and she was the littlest, and you know what men are, and the short and long of it is that she was hung up in a basket.

It was rough and simple, and not unlike what baby bears would have made of an underground house in the same circumstances. But there was one recess in the wall, no larger than a bird-cage, which was the private apartment of Tinker Bo. It could be shut off from the rest of the house by a tiny curtain, which Tink, who was most fastidious and bed-chamber combined. The couch, as he always called it, was a genuine King Mab, with club legs; and he varied the bedspreads according to what fruit-blossom was in season. His mirror was a Puss-in-Boots, of which there are now only three, unchipped, known to faery dealers; the washstand was Pie-crust and reversible, the breast of drawers an authentic Charming the Sixth, and the carpet and rugs the best (the early) period of Margery and Robin. There was a chandelier from Tiddlywinks for the look of the thing, but of course he lit the residence himself. Tink was very contemptuous of the rest of the house, as indeed was perhaps inevitable, and his chamber, though handsome, looked rather conceited, having the appearance of a nose permanently turned up.

I suppose it was all especially entrancing to Walter, because those rampagious girls of his gave him so much to do. Really there were whole weeks when, except perhaps with a stocking in the evening, he was never above ground. The cooking, I can tell you, kept his nose to the pot, and even if there was nothing in it, even if there was no pot, he had to keep watching that it came aboil just the same. You never exactly knew whether there would be a real meal or just a make-believe, it all depended upon Patty's whim: she could eat, really eat, if it was part of a game, but she could not stodge, which is what most children like better than anything else; the next best thing being to talk about it. Make-believe was so real to her that during a meal of it you could see her getting rounder. Of course it was trying, but you simply had to follow her lead, and if you could prove to her that you were getting loose for your tree she let you stodge.

Walter's favourite time for sewing and darning was after they had all gone to bed. Then, as he expressed it, he had a breathing time for himself; and he occupied it in making new things for them, and putting double pieces on the knees, for they were all most frightfully hard on their knees.

When he sat down to a basketful of their stockings, every heel with a hole in it, he would fling up his arms and exclaim, "Oh dear, I am sure I sometimes think bachelors are to be envied!"

His face beamed when he exclaimed this.

You remember about his pet wolf. Well, it very soon discovered that he had come to the island and it found him out, and they just ran into each other's arms. After that it followed him about everywhere.

As time wore on did he think much about the beloved parents he had left behind him? This is a difficult question, because it is quite impossible to say how time does wear on in the Neverland, where it is calculated by moons and suns, and there are ever so many more of them than on the mainland. But I am afraid that Walter did not really worry about his mother and father; he was absolutely confident that they would always keep the window open for him to fly back by, and this gave him complete ease of mind. What did disturb him at times was that Joanie remembered her parents vaguely only, as people she had once known, while Michelle was quite willing to believe that he was really her father. These things scared him a little, and nobly anxious to do his duty, he tried to fix the old life in their minds by setting them examination papers on it, as like as possible to the ones he used to do at school. The other girls thought this awfully interesting, and insisted on joining, and they made slates for themselves, and sat round the table, writing and thinking hard about the questions he had written on another slate and passed round. They were the most ordinary questions -- "What was the colour of Father's eyes? Which was taller, Mother or Father? Was Father blonde or brunette? Answer all three questions if possible." "(A) Write an essay of not less than 40 words on How I spent my last Holidays, or The Characters of Mother and Father compared. Only one of these to be attempted." Or "(1) Describe Father's laugh; (2) Describe Mother's laugh; (3) Describe Father's Party Dress; (4) Describe the Kennel and its Inmate."

They were just everyday questions like these, and when you could not answer them you were told to make a cross; and it was really dreadful what a number of crosses even Joanie made. Of course the only girl who replied to every question was Slightly, and no one could have been more hopeful of coming out first, but her answers were perfectly ridiculous, and she really came out last: a melancholy thing.

Patty did not compete. For one thing she despised all fathers except Walter, and for another she was the only girl on the island who could neither write nor spell; not the smallest word. She was above all that sort of thing.

By the way, the questions were all written in the past tense. What was the colour of Father's eyes, and so on. Walter, you see, had been forgetting, too.

Adventures, of course, as we shall see, were of daily occurrence; but about this time Patty invented, with Walter's help, a new game that fascinated her enormously, until she suddenly had no more interest in it, which, as you have been told, was what always happened with her games. It consisted in pretending not to have adventures, in doing the sort of thing Joanie and Michelle had been doing all their lives, sitting on stools flinging balls in the air, pushing each other, going out for walks and coming back without having killed so much as a grizzly. To see Patty doing nothing on a stool was a great sight; she could not help looking solemn at such times, to sit still seemed to her such a comic thing to do. She boasted that she had gone walking for the good of her health. For several suns these were the most novel of all adventures to her; and Joanie and Michelle had to pretend to be delighted also; otherwise she would have treated them severely.

She often went out alone, and when she came back you were never absolutely certain whether she had had an adventure or not. She might have forgotten it so completely that she said nothing about it; and then when you went out you found the body; and, on the other hand, she might say a great deal about it, and yet you could not find the body. Sometimes she came home with her head bandaged, and then Walter cooed over her and bathed it in lukewarm water, while she told a dazzling tale. But he was never quite sure, you know. There were, however, many adventures which he knew to be true because he was in them himself, and there were still more that were at least partly true, for the other girls were in them and said they were wholly true. To describe them all would require a book as large as an English-Latin, Latin-English Dictionary, and the most we can do is to give one as a specimen of an average hour on the island. The difficulty is which one to choose. Should we take the brush with the redskins at Slightly Gulch? It was a sanguinary affair, and especially interesting as showing one of Patty's peculiarities, which was that in the middle of a fight she would suddenly change sides. At the Gulch, when victory was still in the balance, sometimes leaning this way and sometimes that, she called out, "I'm redskin to-day; what are you,

Tootles?" And Tootles answered, "Redskin; what are you, Nibs?" and Nibs said, "Redskin; what are you Twin?" and so on; and they were all redskins; and of course this would have ended the fight had not the real redskins fascinated by Patty's methods, agreed to be lost girls for that once, and so at it they all went again, more fiercely than ever.

The extraordinary upshot of this adventure was -- but we have not decided yet that this is the adventure we are to narrate. Perhaps a better one would be the night attack by the redskins on the house under the ground, when several of them stuck in the hollow trees and had to be pulled out like corks. Or we might tell how Patty saved Tiger Claw's life in the Mermen' Lagoon, and so made him her ally.

Or we could tell of that cake the pirates cooked so that the girls might eat it and perish; and how they placed it in one cunning spot after another; but always Walter snatched it from the hands of his children, so that in time it lost its succulence, and became as hard as a stone, and was used as a missile, and Hook fell over it in the dark.

Or suppose we tell of the birds that were Patty's friends, particularly of the Never bird that built in a tree overhanging the lagoon, and how the nest fell into the water, and still the bird sat on his eggs, and Patty gave orders that he was not to be disturbed. That is a pretty story, and the end shows how grateful a bird can be; but if we tell it we must also tell the whole adventure of the lagoon, which would of course be telling two adventures rather than just one. A shorter adventure, and quite as exciting, was Tinker Bo's attempt, with the help of some street faeries, to have the sleeping Walter conveyed on a great floating leaf to the mainland. Fortunately the leaf gave way and Walter woke, thinking it was bath-time, and swam back. Or again, we might choose Patty's defiance of the lionesses, when she drew a circle round her on the ground with an arrow and dared them to cross it; and though she waited for hours, with the other girls and Walter looking on breathlessly from trees, not one of them dared to accept her challenge.

Which of these adventures shall we choose? The best way will be to toss for it.

I have tossed, and the lagoon has won. This al-most makes one wish that the gulch or the cake or Tink's leaf had won. Of course I could do it again, and make it best out of three; however, per-haps fairest to stick to the lagoon.

Chapter 8 THE MERMEN'S LAGOON

If you shut your eyes and are a lucky one, you may see at times a shapeless pool of lovely pale colours suspended in the darkness; then if you squeeze your eyes tighter, the pool begins to take shape, and the colours become so vivid that with another squeeze they must go on fire. But just before they go on fire you see the lagoon. This is the nearest you ever get to it on the mainland, just one heavenly moment; if there could be two moments you might see the surf and hear the mermen singing.

The children often spent long summer days on this lagoon, swimming or floating most of the time, playing the merman games in the water, and so forth. You must not think from this that the mermen were on friendly terms with them: on the contrary, it was among Walter's lasting regrets that all the time he was on the island he never had a civil word from one of them. When he stole softly to the edge of the lagoon he might see them by the score, especially on Marooners' Rock, where they loved to bask, combing out their hair in a lazy way that quite irritated him; or he might even swim, on tiptoe as it were, to within a yard of them, but then they saw him and dived, probably splashing him with their tails, not by accident, but intentionally.

They treated all the girls in the same way, except of course Patty, who chatted with them on Marooners' Rock by the hour, and sat on their tails when they got cheeky. She gave Walter one of their combs.

The most haunting time at which to see them is at the turn of the moon, when they utter strange wailing cries; but the lagoon is dangerous for mortals then, and until the evening of which we have now to tell, Walter had never seen the lagoon by moonlight, less from fear, for of course Patty would have accompanied him, than because he had strict rules about every one being in bed by seven. He was often at the lagoon, however, on sunny days after rain, when the mermen come up in extraordinary numbers to play with their bubbles. The bubbles of many colours made in rainbow water they treat as balls, hitting them gaily from one to another with their tails, and trying to keep them in the rainbow till they burst. The goals are at each end of the rainbow, and the keepers only are allowed to use their hands. Sometimes a dozen of these games will be going on in the lagoon at a time, and it is quite a pretty sight.

But the moment the children tried to join in they had to play by themselves, for the mermen immediately disappeared. Nevertheless we have proof that they secretly watched the interlopers, and were not above taking an idea from them; for Joanie introduced a new way of hitting the bubble, with the head instead of the hand, and the mermen adopted it. This is the one mark that Joanie has left on the Neverland.

It must also have been rather pretty to see the children resting on a rock for half an hour after their mid-day meal. Walter insisted on their doing this, and it had to be a real rest even though the meal was make-believe. So they lay there in the sun, and their bodies glistened in it, while he sat beside them and looked important.

It was one such day, and they were all on Marooners' Rock. The rock was not much larger than their great bed, but of course they all knew how not to take up much room, and they were dozing, or at least lying with their eyes shut, and pinching occasionally when they thought Walter was not looking. He was very busy, stitching.

While he stitched a change came to the lagoon. Little shivers ran over it, and the sun went away and shadows stole across the water, turning it cold. Walter could no longer see to thread his needle, and when he looked up, the lagoon that had always hitherto been such a laughing place seemed formidable and unfriendly.

It was not, he knew, that night had come, but something as dark as night had come. No, worse than that. It had not come, but it had sent that shiver through the sea to say that it was coming. What was it?

There crowded upon him all the stories he had been told of Marooners' Rock, so called because evil captains put sailors on it and leave them there to drown. They drown when the tide rises, for then it is submerged.

Of course he should have roused the children at once; not merely because of the unknown that was stalking toward them, but because it was no longer good for them to sleep on a rock grown chilly. But he was a young father and he did not know this; he thought you simply must stick to your rule about half an hour after the mid-day meal. So, though fear was upon him, and he longed to hear female voices, he would not waken them. Even when he heard the sound of muffled oars, though his heart was in his mouth, he did not waken them. He stood over them to let them have their sleep out. Was it not brave of Walter?

It was well for those girls then that there was one among them who could sniff danger even in her sleep. Patty sprang erect, as wide awake at once as a dog, and with one warning cry she roused the others.

She stood motionless, one hand to her ear.

"Pirates!" she cried. The others came closer to her. A strange smile was playing about her face, and Walter saw it and shuddered. While that smile was on her face no one dared address her; all they could do was to stand ready to obey. The order came sharp and incisive.

"Dive!"

There was a gleam of legs, and instantly the lagoon seemed deserted. Marooners' Rock stood alone in the forbidding waters as if it were itself marooned.

The boat drew nearer. It was the pirate dinghy, with three figures in him, Smee and Starkey, and the third a captive, no other than Tiger Claw. His hands and ankles were tied, and he knew what was to be his fate. He was to be left on the rock to perish, an end to one of his race more terrible than death by fire or torture, for is it not written in the book of the tribe that there is no path through water to the happy hunting-ground? Yet his face was impassive; he was the son of a chief, he must die as a chief's son, it is enough.

They had caught him boarding the pirate ship with a knife in his mouth. No watch was kept on the ship, it being Hook's boast that the wind of her name guarded the ship for a mile around. Now his fate would help to guard it also. One more wail would go the round in that wind by night.

In the gloom that they brought with them the two pirates did not see the rock till they crashed into it.

"Luff, you lubber," cried an Irish voice that was Smee's; "here's the rock. Now, then, what we have to do is to hoist the redskin on to it and leave him here to drown."

It was the work of one brutal moment to land the handsome boy on the rock; he was too proud to offer a vain resistance.

Quite near the rock, but out of sight, two heads were bobbing up and down, Patty's and Walter's. Walter was crying, for it was the first tragedy he had seen. Patty had seen many tragedies, but she had forgotten them all. She was less sorry than Walter for Tiger Claw: it was two against one that angered her, and she meant to save him. An easy way would have been to wait until the pirates had gone, but she was never one to choose the easy way.

There was almost nothing she could not do, and she now imitated the voice of Hook.

"Ahoy there, you lubbers!" she called. It was a marvellous imitation.

"The captain!" said the pirates, staring at each other in surprise.

"She must be swimming out to us," Starkey said, when they had looked for her in vain.

"We are putting the redskin on the rock," Smee called out.

"Set him free," came the astonishing answer.

"Free!"

"Yes, cut his bonds and let him go."

"But, captain -- "

"At once, d'ye hear," cried Patty, "or I'll plunge my hook in you."

"This is queer!" Smee gasped.

"Better do what the captain orders," said Starkey nervously.

"Ay, ay." Smee said, and she cut Tiger Claw's cords. At once like an eel he slid between Starkey's legs into the water.

Of course Walter was very elated over Patty's cleverness; but he knew that she would be elated also and very likely crow and thus betray herself, so at once his hand went out to cover her mouth. But it was stayed even in the act, for "Boat ahoy!" rang over the lagoon in Hook's voice, and this time it was not Patty who had spoken.

Patty may have been about to crow, but her face puckered in a whistle of surprise instead.

"Boat ahoy!" again came the voice.

Now Walter understood. The real Hook was also in the water.

She was swimming to the boat, and as her women showed a light to guide her she had soon reached them. In the light of the lantern Walter saw her hook grip the boat's side; he saw her evil swarthy face as she rose dripping from the water, and, quaking, he would have liked to swim away, but Patty would not budge. She was tingling with life and also top-heavy with conceit. "Am I not a wonder, oh, I am a wonder!" she whispered to him, and though he thought so also, he was really glad for the sake of her reputation that no one heard her except himself.

She signed to him to listen.

The two pirates were very curious to know what had brought their captain to them, but she sat with her head on her hook in a position of profound melancholy.

"Captain, is all well?" they asked timidly, but she answered with a hollow moan.

"She sighs," said Smee.

"She sighs again," said Starkey.

"And yet a third time she sighs," said Smee.

Then at last she spoke passionately.

"The game's up," she cried, "those girls have found a father."

Affrighted though he was, Walter swelled with pride.

"O evil day!" cried Starkey.

"What's a father?" asked the ignorant Smee.

Walter was so shocked that he exclaimed. "She doesn't know!" and always after this he felt that if you could have a pet pirate Smee would be his one.

Patty pulled him beneath the water, for Hook had started up, crying, "What was that?"

"I heard nothing," said Starkey, raising the lantern over the waters, and as the pirates looked they saw a strange sight. It was the nest I have told you of, floating on the lagoon, and the Never bird was sitting on it.

"See," said Hook in answer to Smee's question, "that is a father. What a lesson! The nest must have fallen into the water, but would the father desert his eggs? No."

There was a break in her voice, as if for a moment she recalled innocent days when -- but she brushed away this weakness with her hook.

Smee, much impressed, gazed at the bird as the nest was borne past, but the more suspicious Starkey said, "If he is a father, perhaps he is hanging about here to help Patty."

Hook winced. "Ay," she said, "that is the fear that haunts me."

She was roused from this dejection by Smee's eager voice.

"Captain," said Smee, "could we not kidnap these girls' father and make him our father?"

"It is a princessly scheme," cried Hook, and at once it took practical shape in her great brain. "We will seize the children and carry them to the boat: the girls we will make walk the plank, and Walter shall be our father."

Again Walter forgot himself.

"Never!" he cried, and bobbed.

"What was that?"

But they could see nothing. They thought it must have been a leaf in the wind. "Do you agree, my bullies?" asked Hook.

"There is my hand on it," they both said.

"And there is my hook. Swear."

They all swore. By this time they were on the rock, and suddenly Hook remembered Tiger Claw.

"Where is the redskin?" she demanded abruptly.

She had a playful humour at moments, and they thought this was one of the moments.

"That is all right, captain," Smee answered complacently; "we let him go."

"Let him go!" cried Hook.

"'Twas your own orders," the bo'sun faltered.

"You called over the water to us to let him go," said Starkey.

"Brimstone and gall," thundered Hook, "what cozening is going on here!" Her face had gone black with rage, but she saw that they believed their words, and she was startled. "Lasses," she said, shaking a little, "I gave no such order."

"It is passing queer," Smee said, and they all fidgeted uncomfortably. Hook raised her voice, but there was a quiver in it.

"Spirit that haunts this dark lagoon to-night," she cried, "dost hear me?"

Of course Patty should have kept quiet, but of course she did not. She immediately answered in Hook's voice:

"Odds, bobs, hammer and tongs, I hear you."

In that supreme moment Hook did not blanch, even at the gills, but Smee and Starkey clung to each other in terror.

"Who are you, stranger? Speak!" Hook demanded.

"I am James Hook," replied the voice, "captain of the JOLLY ROGER."

"You are not; you are not," Hook cried hoarsely.

"Brimstone and gall," the voice retorted, "say that again, and I'll cast anchor in you."

Hook tried a more ingratiating manner. "If you are Hook," she said almost humbly, "come tell me, who am I?"

"A codfish," replied the voice, "only a codfish."

"A codfish!" Hook echoed blankly, and it was then, but not till then, that her proud spirit broke. She saw her women draw back from her.

"Have we been captained all this time by a codfish!" they muttered. "It is lowering to our pride."

They were her dogs snapping at her, but, tragic figure though she had become, she scarcely heeded them. Against such fearful evidence it was not their belief in her that she needed, it was her own. She felt her ego slipping from her. "Don't desert me, bully," she whispered hoarsely to it.

In her dark nature there was a touch of the masculine, as in all the great pirates, and it sometimes gave her intuitions. Suddenly she tried the guessing game.

"Hook," she called, "have you another voice?"

Now Patty could never resist a game, and she answered blithely in her own voice, "I have."

"And another name?"

"Ay, ay."

"Vegetable?" asked Hook.

"No."

"Mineral?"

"No."

"Animal?"

"Yes."

"Woman?"

"No!" This answer rang out scornfully.

"Girl?"

"Yes."

"Ordinary girl?"

"No!"

"Wonderful girl?"

To Walter's pain the answer that rang out this time was "Yes."

"Are you in England?"

"No."

"Are you here?"

"Yes."

Hook was completely puzzled. "You ask her some questions," she said to the others, wiping her damp brow.

Smee reflected. "I can't think of a thing," she said regretfully.

"Can't guess, can't guess!" crowed Patty. "Do you give it up?"

Of course in her pride she was carrying the game too far, and the miscreants saw their chance.

"Yes, yes," they answered eagerly.

"Well, then," she cried, "I am Patty Pan."

Pan!

In a moment Hook was herself again, and Smee and Starkey were her faithful henchmen.

"Now we have her," Hook shouted. "Into the water, Smee. Starkey, mind the boat. Take her dead or alive!"

She leaped as she spoke, and simultaneously came the gay voice of Patty.

"Are you ready, girls?"

"Ay, ay," from various parts of the lagoon.

"Then lam into the pirates."

The fight was short and sharp. First to draw blood was Joanie, who gallantly climbed into the boat and held Starkey. There was fierce struggle, in which the cutlass was torn from the pirate's grasp. She wriggled overboard and Joanie leapt after her. The dinghy drifted away.

Here and there a head bobbed up in the water, and there was a flash of steel followed by a cry or a whoop. In the confusion some struck at their own side. The corkscrew of Smee got Tootles in the fourth rib, but she was herself pinked in turn by Curly. Farther from the rock Starkey was pressing Slightly and the twins hard.

Where all this time was Patty? She was seeking bigger game.

The others were all brave girls, and they must not be blamed for backing from the pirate captain. Her iron claw made a circle of dead water round her, from which they fled like affrighted fishes.

But there was one who did not fear her: there was one prepared to enter that circle.

Strangely, it was not in the water that they met. Hook rose to the rock to breathe, and at the same moment Patty scaled it on the opposite side. The rock was slippery as a ball, and they had to crawl rather than climb. Neither knew that the other was coming. Each feeling for a grip met the other's arm: in surprise they raised their heads; their faces were almost touching; so they met.

Some of the greatest heroes have confessed that just before they fell to. Had it been so with Patty at that moment I would admit it. After all, she was the only woman that the Sea-Cook had feared. But Patty had no sinking, she had one feeling only, gladness; and she gnashed her pretty teeth with joy. Quick as thought she snatched a knife from Hook's belt and was about to drive it home, when she saw that she was higher up the rock that her foe. It would not have been fighting fair. She gave the pirate a hand to help her up.

It was then that Hook bit her.

Not the pain of this but its unfairness was what dazed Patty. It made her quite helpless. She could only stare, horrified. Every child is affected thus the first time she is treated unfairly. All she thinks she has a right to when she comes to you to be yours is fairness. After you have been unfair to her she will love you again, but will never afterwards be quite the same girl. No one ever gets over the first unfairness; no one except Patty. She often met it, but she always forgot it. I suppose that was the real difference between her and all the rest.

So when she met it now it was like the first time; and she could just stare, helpless. Twice the iron hand clawed her.

A few moments afterwards the other girls saw Hook in the water striking wildly for the ship; no elation on the pestilent face now, only white fear, for the crocodile was in dogged pursuit of her. On ordinary occasions the girls would have swum alongside cheering; but now they were uneasy, for they had lost both Patty and Walter, and were scouring the lagoon for them, calling them by name. They found the dinghy and went home in it, shouting "Patty, Walter" as they went, but no answer came save mocking laughter from the mermen. "They must be swimming back or flying," the girls concluded. They were not very anxious, because they had such faith in Patty. They chuckled, boylike, because they would be late for bed; and it was all father Walter's fault!

When their voices died away there came cold silence over the lagoon, and then a feeble cry.

"Help, help!"

Two small figures were beating against the rock; the boy had fainted and lay on the girl's arm. With a last effort Patty pulled him up the rock and then lay down beside him. Even as she also fainted she saw that the water was rising. She knew that they would soon be drowned, but she could do no more.

As they lay side by side a merman caught Walter by the feet, and began pulling him softly into the water. Patty, feeling him slip from her, woke with a start, and was just in time to draw him back. But she had to tell him the truth.

"We are on the rock, Walter," she said, "but it is growing smaller. Soon the water will be over it."

He did not understand even now.

"We must go," he said, almost brightly.

"Yes," she answered faintly.

"Shall we swim or fly, Patty?"

She had to tell him.

"Do you think you could swim or fly as far as the island, Walter, without my help?"

He had to admit that he was too tired.

She moaned.

"What is it?" he asked, anxious about her at once.

"I can't help you, Walter. Hook wounded me. I can neither fly nor swim."

"Do you mean we shall both be drowned?"

"Look how the water is rising."

They put their hands over their eyes to shut out the sight. They thought they would soon be no more. As they sat thus something brushed against Patty as light as a kiss, and stayed there, as if saying timidly, "Can I be of any use?"

It was the tail of a kite, which Michelle had made some days before. It had torn itself out of her hand and floated away.

"Michelle's kite," Patty said without interest, but next moment she had seized the tail, and was pulling the kite toward her.

"It lifted Michelle off the ground," she cried; "why should it not carry you?"

"Both of us!"

"It can't lift two; Michelle and Curly tried."

"Let us draw lots," Walter said bravely.

"And you a lord; never." Already she had tied the tail round him. He clung to her; he refused to go without her; but with a "Good-bye, Walter," she pushed him from the rock; and in a few minutes he was borne out of her sight. Patty was alone on the lagoon.

The rock was very small now; soon it would be submerged. Pale rays of light tiptoed across the waters; and by and by there was to be heard a sound at once the most musical and the most melancholy in the world: the mermen calling to the moon.

Patty was not quite like other girls; but she was afraid at last. A tremour ran through her, like a shudder passing over the sea; but on the sea one shudder follows another till there are hundreds of them, and Patty felt just the one. Next moment she was standing erect on the rock again, with that smile on her face and a drum beating within her. It was saying, "To die will be an awfully big adventure."

Chapter 9 THE NEVER BIRD

The last sound Patty heard before she was quite alone were the mermen retiring one by one to their bedchambers under the sea. She was too far away to hear their doors shut; but every door in the coral caves where they live rings a tiny bell when it opens or closes (as in all the nicest houses on the mainland), and she heard the bells.

Steadily the waters rose till they were nibbling at her feet; and to pass the time until they made their final gulp, she watched the only thing on the lagoon. She thought it was a piece of floating paper, perhaps part of the kite, and wondered idly how long it would take to drift ashore.

Presently she noticed as an odd thing that it was undoubtedly out upon the lagoon with some definite purpose, for it was fighting the tide, and sometimes winning; and when it won, Patty, always sympathetic to the weaker side, could not help clapping; it was such a gallant piece of paper.

It was not really a piece of paper; it was the Never bird, making desperate efforts to reach Patty on the nest. By working his wings, in a way he had learned since the nest fell into the water, he was able to some extent to guide his strange craft, but by the time Patty recognised him he was very exhausted. He had come to save her, to give her his nest, though there were eggs in it. I rather wonder at the bird, for though she had been nice to him, she had also sometimes tormented him. I can suppose only that, like Mr. Darling and the rest of them, he was melted because she had all her first teeth.

He called out to her what he had come for, and she called out to him what he was doing there; but of course neither of them understood the other's language. In fanciful stories people can talk to the birds freely, and I wish for the moment I could pretend that this were such a story, and say that Patty replied intelligently to the Never bird; but truth is best, and I want to tell you only what really happened. Well, not only could they not understand each other, but they forgot their manners.

"I -- want -- you -- to -- get -- into -- the -- nest," the bird called, speaking as slowly and distinctly as possible, "and -- then -- you -- can -- drift -- ashore, but -- I -- am -- too -- tired -- to -- bring -- it -- any -- nearer -- so -- you -- must -- try to -- swim -- to -- it."

"What are you quacking about?" Patty answered. "Why don't you let the nest drift as usual?"

"I -- want -- you -- " the bird said, and repeated it all over.

Then Patty tried slow and distinct.

"What -- are -- you -- quacking -- about?" and so on.

The Never bird became irritated; they have very short tempers.

"You dunderheaded little jay," he screamed, "Why don't you do as I tell you?"

Patty felt that he was calling her names, and at a venture she retorted hotly:

"So are you!"

Then rather curiously they both snapped out the same remark:

"Shut up!"

"Shut up!"

Nevertheless the bird was determined to save her if he could, and by one last mighty effort he propelled the nest against the rock. Then up he flew; deserting his eggs, so as to make his meaning clear.

Then at last she understood, and clutched the nest and waved her thanks to the bird as he fluttered overhead. It was not to receive her thanks, however, that he hung there in the sky; it was not even to watch her get into the nest; it was to see what she did with his eggs.

There were two large white eggs, and Patty lifted them up and reflected. The bird covered his face with his wings, so as not to see the last of them; but he could not help peeping between the feathers.

I forget whether I have told you that there was a stave on the rock, driven into it by some buccaneers of long ago to mark the site of buried treasure. The children had discovered the glittering hoard, and when in a mischievous mood used to fling showers of moidores, diamonds, pearls and pieces of eight to the gulls, who pounced upon them for food, and then flew away, raging at the scurvy trick that had been played upon them. The stave was still there, and on it Starkey had hung her hat, a deep tarpaulin, watertight, with a broad brim. Patty put the eggs into this hat and set it on the lagoon. It floated handsomely.

The Never bird saw at once what she was up to, and screamed his admiration of her; and, alas, Patty crowed her agreement with him. Then she got into the nest, reared the stave in it as a mast, and hung up her blouse for a sail. At the same moment the bird fluttered down upon the hat and once more sat snugly on his eggs. He drifted in one direction, and she was borne off in another, both cheering.

Of course when Patty landed she beached her barque in a place where the bird would easily find it; but the hat was such a great success that he abandoned the nest. It drifted about till it went to pieces, and often Starkey came to the shore of the lagoon, and with many bitter feelings watched the bird sitting on her hat. As we shall not see him again, it may be worth mentioning here that all Never birds now build in that shape of nest, with a broad brim on which the youngsters take an airing.

Great were the rejoicings when Patty reached the home under the ground almost as soon as Walter, who had been carried hither and thither by the kite. Every girl had adventures to tell; but perhaps the biggest adventure of all was that they were several hours late for bed. This so inflated them that they did various dodgy things to get staying up still longer, such as demanding bandages; but Walter, though glorying in having them all home again safe and sound, was scandalised by the lateness of the hour, and cried, "To bed, to bed," in a voice that had to be obeyed. Next day, however, he was awfully tender, and gave out

bandages to every one, and they played till bedtime at limping about and carrying their arms in
slings.

Chapter 10 THE HAPPY HOME

One important result of the brush on the lagoon was that it made the redskins their friends. Patty had saved Tiger Claw from a dreadful fate, and now there was nothing he and his braves would not do for her. All night they sat above, keeping watch over the home under the ground and awaiting the big attack by the pirates which obviously could not be much longer delayed. Even by day they hung about, smoking the pipe of peace, and looking almost as if they wanted tit-bits to eat.

They called Patty the Great White Mother, prostrating themselves before her; and she liked this tremendously, so that it was not really good for her.

"The great white mother," she would say to them in a very gentleladyly manner, as they grovelled at her feet, "is glad to see the Piccaninny warriors protecting her wigwam from the pirates."

"Me Tiger Claw," that lovely creature would reply. "Patty Pan save me, me her velly nice friend. Me no let pirates hurt her."

He was far too pretty to cringe in this way, but Patty thought it her due, and she would answer condescendingly, "It is good. Patty Pan has spoken."

Always when she said, "Patty Pan has spoken," it meant that they must now shut up, and they accepted it humbly in that spirit; but they were by no means so respectful to the other girls, whom they looked upon as just ordinary braves. They said "How-do?" to them, and things like that; and what annoyed the girls was that Patty seemed to think this all right.

Secretly Walter sympathised with them a little, but he was far too loyal a housewife to listen to any complaints against mother. "Mother knows best," he always said, whatever his private opinion must be. His private opinion was that the redskins should not call him a squaw.

We have now reached the evening that was to be known among them as the Night of Nights, because of its adventures and their upshot. The day, as if quietly gathering its forces, had been almost uneventful, and now the redskins in their blankets were at their posts above, while, below, the children were having their evening meal; all except Patty, who had gone out to get the time. The way you got the time on the island was to find the crocodile, and then stay near her till the clock struck.

The meal happened to be a make-believe tea, and they sat around the board, guzzling in their greed; and really, what with their chatter and recriminations, the noise, as Walter said, was positively deafening. To be sure, he did not mind noise, but he simply would not have them grabbing things, and then excusing themselves by saying that Tootles had pushed their elbow. There was a fixed rule that they must never hit back at meals, but should refer the matter of dispute to Walter by raising the right arm politely and saying, "I complain of so-and-so;" but what usually happened was that they forgot to do this or did it too much.

"Silence," cried Walter when for the twentieth time he had told them that they were not all to speak at once. "Is your mug empty, Slightly darling?"

"Not quite empty, mummy," Slightly said, after looking into an imaginary mug.

"She hasn't even begun to drink her milk," Nibs interposed.

This was telling, and Slightly seized her chance.

"I complain of Nibs," she cried promptly.

Joanie, however, had held up her hand first.

"Well, Joanie?"

"May I sit in Patty's chair, as she is not here?"

"Sit in mother's chair, Joanie!" Walter was scandalised. "Certainly not."

"She is not really our mother," Joanie answered. "She didn't even know how a mother does till I showed her."

This was grumbling. "We complain of Joanie," cried the twins.

Tootles held up her hand. She was so much the humblest of them, indeed she was the only humble one, that Walter was specially gentle with her.

"I don't suppose," Tootles said diffidently, "that I could be mother."

"No, Tootles."

Once Tootles began, which was not very often, she had a silly way of going on.

"As I can't be mother," she said heavily, "I don't suppose, Michelle, you would let me be baby?"

"No, I won't," Michelle rapped out. She was already in her basket.

"As I can't be baby," Tootles said, getting heavier and heavier and heavier, "do you think I could be a twin?"

"No, indeed," replied the twins; "it's awfully difficult to be a twin."

"As I can't be anything important," said Tootles, "would any of you like to see me do a trick?"

"No," they all replied.

Then at last she stopped. "I hadn't really any hope," she said.

The hateful telling broke out again.

"Slightly is coughing on the table."

"The twins began with cheese-cakes."

"Curly is taking both butter and honey."

"Nibs is speaking with her mouth full."

"I complain of the twins."

"I complain of Curly."

"I complain of Nibs."

"Oh dear, oh dear," cried Walter, "I'm sure I sometimes think that bachelors are to be envied."

He told them to clear away, and sat down to his work-basket, a heavy load of stockings and every knee with a hole in it as usual.

"Walter," remonstrated Michelle, "I'm too big for a cradle."

"I must have somebody in a cradle," he said almost tartly, "and you are the littlest. A cradle is such a nice homely thing to have about a house."

While he sewed they played around him; such a group of happy faces and dancing limbs lit up by that romantic fire. It had become a very familiar scene, this, in the home under the ground, but we are looking on it for the last time.

There was a step above, and Walter, you may be sure, was the first to recognize it.

"Children, I hear your mother's step. She likes you to meet her at the door."

Above, the redskins crouched before Patty.

"Watch well, braves. I have spoken."

And then, as so often before, the gay children dragged her from her tree. As so often before, but never again.

She had brought nuts for the girls as well as the correct time for Walter.

"Patty, you just spoil them, you know," Walter simpered.

"Ah, old lord," said Patty, hanging up her gun.

"It was me told her fathers are called old lord," Michelle whispered to Curly.

"I complain of Michelle," said Curly instantly.

The first twin came to Patty. "Mother, we want to dance."

"Dance away, my little woman," said Patty, who was in high good humour.

"But we want you to dance."

Patty was really the best dancer among them, but she pretended to be scandalised.

"Me! My old bones would rattle!"

"And mummy too."

"What," cried Walter, "the father of such an armful, dance!"

"But on a Saturday night," Slightly insinuated.

It was not really Saturday night, at least it may have been, for they had long lost count of the days; but always if they wanted to do anything special they said this was Saturday night, and then they did it.

"Of course it is Saturday night, Patty," Walter said, relenting.

"People of our figure, Walter!"

"But it is only among our own progeny."

"True, true."

So they were told they could dance, but they must put on their nighties first.

"Ah, old lord," Patty said aside to Walter, warming herself by the fire and looking down at him as he sat turning a heel, "there is nothing more pleasant of an evening for you and me when the day's toil is over than to rest by the fire with the little ones near by."

"It is sweet, Patty, isn't it?" Walter said, frightfully gratified. "Patty, I think Curly has your nose."

"Michelle takes after you."

He went to her and put his hand on her shoulder.

"Dear Patty," he said, "with such a large family, of course, I have now passed my best, but you don't want tochange me, do you?"

"No, Walter."

Certainly she did not want a change, but she looked at him uncomfortably, blinking, you know, like one not sure whether she was awake or asleep.

"Patty, what is it?"

"I was just thinking," she said, a little scared. "It is only make-believe, isn't it, that I am their mother?"

"Oh yes," Walter said primly.

"You see," she continued apologetically, "it would make me seem so old to be their real mother."

"But they are ours, Patty, yours and mine."

"But not really, Walter?" she asked anxiously.

"Not if you don't wish it," he replied; and he distinctly heard her sigh of relief. "Patty," he asked, trying to speak firmly, "what are your exact feelings to me?"

"Those of a devoted daughter, Walter."

"I thought so," he said, and went and sat by himself at the extreme end of the room.

"You are so queer," she said, frankly puzzled, "and Tiger Claw is just the same. There is something he wants to be to me, but he says it is not my father."

"No, indeed, it is not," Walter replied with frightful emphasis. Now we know why he was prejudiced against the redskins.

"Then what is it?"

"It isn't for a lord to tell."

"Oh, very well," Patty said, a little nettled. "Perhaps Tinker Bo will tell me."

"Oh yes, Tinker Bo will tell you," Walter retorted scornfully. "He is an abandoned little creature."

Here Tink, who was in his bedroom, eavesdropping, squeaked out something impudent.

"He says he glories in being abandoned," Patty interpreted.

She had a sudden idea. "Perhaps Tink wants to be my father?"

"You silly ass!" cried Tinker Bo in a passion.

He had said it so often that Walter needed no translation.

"I almost agree with him," Walter snapped. Fancy Walter snapping! But he had been much tried, and he little knew what was to happen before the night was out. If he had known he would not have snapped.

None of them knew. Perhaps it was best not to know. Their ignorance gave them one more glad hour; and as it was to be their last hour on the island, let us rejoice that there were sixty glad minutes in it. They sang and danced in their night-tunics. Such a deliciously creepy song it was, in which they pretended to be frightened at their own shadows, little witting that so soon shadows would close in upon them, from whom they would shrink in real fear. So uproariously gay was the dance, and how they buffeted each other on the bed and out of it! It was a pillow fight rather than a dance, and when it was finished, the pillows insisted on one bout more, like partners who know that they may never meet again. The stories they told, before it was time for

Walter's good-night story! Even Slightly tried to tell a story that night, but the beginning was so fearfully dull that it appalled not only the others but herself, and she said happily:

"Yes, it is a dull beginning. I say, let us pretend that it is the end."

And then at last they all got into bed for Walter's story, the story they loved best, the story Patty hated. Usually when he began to tell this story she left the room or put her hands over her ears; and possibly if she had done either of those things this time they might all still be on the island. But to-night she remained on her stool; and we shall see what happened.

Chapter 11 WALTER'S STORY

"Listen, then," said Walter, settling down to his story, with Michelle at his feet and seven girls in the bed. "There was once a gentleman -- "

"I had rather she had been a lord," Curly said.

"I wish she had been a white rat," said Nibs.

"Quiet," their father admonished them. "There was a lord also, and -- "

"Oh, mummy," cried the first twin, "you mean that there is a lord also, don't you? He is not dead, is he?"

"Oh, no."

"I am awfully glad he isn't dead," said Tootles. "Are you glad, Joanie?"

"Of course I am."

"Are you glad, Nibs?"

"Rather."

"Are you glad, Twins?"

"We are glad."

"Oh dear," sighed Walter.

"Little less noise there," Patty called out, determined that he should have fair play, however beastly a story it might be in her opinion.

"The gentleman's name," Walter continued, "was Ms. Darling, and his name was Mr. Darling."

"I knew them," Joanie said, to annoy the others.

"I think I knew them," said Michelle rather doubtfully.

"They were married, you know," explained Walter, "and what do you think they had?"

"White rats," cried Nibs, inspired.

"No."

"It's awfully puzzling," said Tootles, who knew the story by heart.

"Quiet, Tootles. They had three descendants."

"What is descendants?"

"Well, you are one, Twin."

"Did you hear that, Joanie? I am a descendant."

"Descendants are only children," said Joanie.

"Oh dear, oh dear," sighed Walter. "Now these three children had a faithful nurse called Norm; but Ms. Darling was angry with him and chained him up in the yard, and so all the children flew away."

"It's an awfully good story," said Nibs.

"They flew away," Walter continued, "to the Neverland, where the lost children are."

"I just thought they did," Curly broke in excitedly. "I don't know how it is, but I just thought they did!"

"O Walter," cried Tootles, "was one of the lost children called Tootles?"

"Yes, she was."

"I am in a story. Hurrah, I am in a story, Nibs."

"Hush. Now I want you to consider the feelings of the unhappy parents with all their children flown away."

"Oo!" they all moaned, though they were not really considering the feelings of the unhappy parents one jot.

"Think of the empty beds!"

"Oo!"

"It's awfully sad," the first twin said cheerfully.

"I don't see how it can have a happy ending," said the second twin. "Do you, Nibs?"

"I'm frightfully anxious."

"If you knew how great is a father's love," Walter told them triumphantly, "you would have no fear." He had now come to the part that Patty hated.

"I do like a father's love," said Tootles, hitting Nibs with a pillow. "Do you like a father's love, Nibs?"

"I do just," said Nibs, hitting back.

"You see," Walter said complacently, "our hero knew that the father would always leave the window open for his children to fly back by; so they stayed away for years and had a lovely time."

"Did they ever go back?"

"Let us now," said Walter, bracing himself up for his finest effort, "take a peep into the future;" and they all gave themselves the twist that makes peeps into the future easier. "Years have rolled by, and who is this elegant lord of uncertain age alighting at London Station?"

"O Walter, who is he?" cried Nibs, every bit as excited as if she didn't know.

"Can it be -- yes -- no -- it is -- the fair Walter!"

"Oh!"

"And who are the two noble portly figures accompanying him, now grown to woman's estate? Can they be Joanie and Michelle? They are!"

"Oh!"

"'See, dear sisters,' says Walter pointing upwards, 'there is the window still standing open. Ah, now we are rewarded for our sublime faith in a father's love.' So up they flew to their mummy and daddy, and pen cannot describe the happy scene, over which we draw a veil."

That was the story, and they were as pleased with it as the fair narrator himself. Everything just as it should be, you see. Off we skip like the most heartless things in the world, which is what children are, but so attractive; and we have an entirely selfish time, and then when we have need of special attention we nobly return for it, confident that we shall be rewarded instead of smacked.

So great indeed was their faith in a father's love that they felt they could afford to be callous for a bit longer.

But there was one there who knew better, and when Walter finished she uttered a hollow groan.

"What is it, Patty?" he cried, running to her, thinking she was ill. He felt her solicitously, lower down than her breast. "Where is it, Patty?"

"It isn't that kind of pain," Patty replied darkly.

"Then what kind is it?"

"Walter, you are wrong about fathers."

They all gathered round her in affright, so alarming was her agitation; and with a fine candour she told them what she had hitherto concealed.

"Long ago," she said, "I thought like you that my father would always keep the window open for me, so I stayed away for moons and moons and moons, and then flew back; but the window was barred, for father had forgotten all about me, and there was another little girl sleeping in my bed."

I am not sure that this was true, but Patty thought it was true; and it scared them.

"Are you sure fathers are like that?"

"Yes."

So this was the truth about fathers. The toads!

Still it is best to be careful; and no one knows so quickly as a child when she should give in. "Walter, let us go home," cried Joanie and Michelle together.

"Yes," he said, clutching them.

"Not to-night?" asked the lost girls bewildered. They knew in what they called their hearts that one can get on quite well without a father, and that it is only the fathers who think you can't.

"At once," Walter replied resolutely, for the horrible thought had come to him: "Perhaps father is in half mourning by this time."

This dread made him forgetful of what must be Patty's feelings, and he said to her rather sharply, "Patty, will you make the necessary arrangements?"

"If you wish it," she replied, as coolly as if he had asked her to pass the nuts.

Not so much as a sorry-to-lose-you between them! If he did not mind the parting, she was going to show him, was Patty, that neither did she.

But of course she cared very much; and she was so full of wrath against grown-ups, who, as usual, were spoiling everything, that as soon as she got inside her tree she breathed intentionally quick short breaths at the rate of about five to a second. She did this because there is a saying in the Neverland that, every time you breathe, a grown-up dies; and Patty was killing them off vindictively as fast as possible.

Then having given the necessary instructions to the redskins she returned to the home, where an unworthy scene had been enacted in her absence. Panic-stricken at the thought of losing Walter the lost girls had advanced upon him threateningly.

"It will be worse than before he came," they cried.

"We shan't let him go."

"Let's keep him prisoner."

"Ay, chain him up."

In his extremity an instinct told him to which of them to turn.

"Tootles," he cried, "I appeal to you."

Was it not strange? He appealed to Tootles, quite the silliest one.

Grandly, however, did Tootles respond. For that one moment she dropped her silliness and spoke with dignity.

"I am just Tootles," she said, "and nobody minds me. But the first who does not behave to Walter like an English gentleman I will blood her severely."

She drew back her hanger; and for that instant her sun was at noon. The others held back uneasily. Then Patty returned, and they saw at once that they would get no support from her. She would keep no boy in the Neverland against his will.

"Walter," she said, striding up and down, "I have asked the redskins to guide you through the wood, as flying tires you so."

"Thank you, Patty."